THE CHURCHILL PAPERS

THE CHURCHILL PAPERS

Leo Kessler

This first world edition published in Great Britain 1998 by
SEVERN HOUSE PUBLISHERS LTD of
9–15 High Street, Sutton, Surrey SM1 1DF.
This first world edition published in the U.S.A. 1998 by
SEVERN HOUSE PUBLISHERS INC of
595 Madison Avenue, New York, N.Y. 10022.

British Library Cataloguing in Publication Data

Kessler, Leo, 1926-
    The Churchill papers
    1. War stories
    I. Title
    823.9'14 [F]

ISBN 0-7278-5397-X

Typeset by Palimpsest Book Production Ltd,
Polmont, Stirlingshire, Scotland.
Printed and bound in Great Britain by
MPG Books Ltd, Bodmin, Cornwall.

Introduction

A MISSION IS PROPOSED

'But what a man! The familiar sound of that voice . . . reminds us again that at rare moments in history, one man of courage and vision can make all the difference, not merely for Britain but for the rest of the world . . . Where and when will Britain or any of us again find such inspiration?'

New York Times on the centenary of
Winston Churchill's birth in 1974

"Welsh git," Yates told himself, drinking secretly from the half of scotch concealed in a brown paper bag. All around him in the big open-plan office, there was no sound save the soft click-click of computers and laptops. No telephone rang (Jenkins had banned their use between twelve and four – *'Nobody in his right mind makes news before four p.m.'*) Conversation, what little there was of it, was subdued, even frightened. Indeed the only sound was that of the news editor Jenkins, 'the Welsh Wizard', as they all called him behind his back, chewing out secretaries, bellowing orders at brow-beaten reporters and constantly barking: "Where's my frigging coffee – black as the devil's heart and one sugar."

Finally, it was Yates's turn to head the new queue which was already beginning to form. Jenkins looked the correspondent up and down, as if he were some particularly disagreeable form of life, noting the nearly new suit, the shining leather shoes, instead of sneakers, and the holdall, marked with fading stickers from Benidorm and Ibiza.

"On the kind of bonus I'll give you if you don't make a balls-up of this, Yates, you'll be able to put on a Southend sticker." He looked at Yates's fat boozer's face and laughed.

As always the 'Welsh Wizard' couldn't resist taking the piss out of anybody when he knew he could get away with it, Yates told himself miserably. Aloud he said, "Ready to go, Chief. Read up all the bumpf last night. Fully in the picture." He rattled off the information, as if he were a well-paid correspondent on the *Sunday Times* with a couple of bestselling books beneath his belt and a big house in London's stockbroker belt.

"Bully for you," Jenkins said, not impressed. He held his

big hornrims – he'd copied them from Robin Day in his heyday – momentarily and glanced at the cribsheet on his littered desk. "Okay, you know the drill. We're flying you – *economy* – to Liège. He'll pick you up there and take you off to that fleapit of the world—"

Yates fumbled for the name of the place, where the ageing Colonel now lived, but Jenkins stopped him with an impatient wave of his hand. Whether he was or not, the news editor always liked to appear as if he was in one hell of a hurry ". . . where he now lives. Remember you've got three days – the paper's not made of money – to get the info we need out of the old guy. At his age, he'll be one of those 'crusty from Cheltenham' old farts. Should be easy to get him to talk. Start with the War. Those guys always love that war of theirs. Remember that at this moment in time."

Yates still had a little sense of style about him after a quarter of a century in Fleet Street so that he winced inwardly at the cliché, but he didn't show his distaste. This assignment, his first foreign one for years, could mean a fat bonus and, if he played his cards right, a nice cushy job on *Panorama*. Then the Welsh Wizard could go and stuff his Welsh leeks up his miserable Welsh arse.

Jenkins thought for a moment, pushing the hornrims to the back of his sleek head. He was doing his 'weary bigshot caught at an unguarded moment' bit, Yates told himself. Then he said, "In essence, we want to know *one*, if there were any truths about those rumours about Churchill back in the fifties. *Two*," he ticked off the number on his tobacco-stained thumb, "what happened to the major players in that caper. *Three*, and most important of all, on account of the fact that those masterminds who read our paper have never heard of Churchill and the rest, if there was any sleaze involved. That's the buzz word, Yates. Get in sleaze

3

any-old-how and we're quids in. Up goes the circulation," he gave Yates that crooked, knowing cynical smile of his, "and my bonus . . . All right, Porkie," he snapped at the overweight sports correspondent, "let's have the poop on the queer soccer guy from Italy – excuse my French, I forget, you call the bastards gay these days, don't we." He blew the embarrassed 'Porkie' a wet kiss. Yates was dismissed. . .

Part One

THE BIG SNATCH

Chapter One

The July afternoon was hot and sultry. Outside, Rome lay dead in the noonday heat. The only sound was the muted tinkle of the tram bells. The Italian capital seemingly slept. The fascist dictator knew why. As always his 'new Romans', as he had once called them proudly, hid in their beds against the oppressive heat – and the defeats now flooding in from the front almost daily. Now the Allies had just landed in Sicily. That would be enough to send them to their beds for a week, hiding between the plump naked breasts of their womenfolk and whores. He grimaced at himself in the ornate Louis Quinze mirror. Why in heaven's name had he been chosen to lead a people like the Italians? What luck his ally and fellow dictator, Hitler, had had in being given his brave Germans to rule. They were peasant boors, who lived off pieces of overcooked pig meat and potatoes, admittedly, but they were brave soldiers to a man. They would never hide behind a woman's skirts. *"Porco de Madonna,"* he growled coarsely, using the peasants' oath, then giving himself a quick spray with perfume to hide the stink of his sweat – Clara, his mistress, wasn't one of those high-born ladies he had often bedded who delighted in the smell of man – he strode out of the little dressing room.

As if he were on parade, he marched across the great hall, his gleaming boots clicking on the marble floor. Here and there an elegant officer snapped to attention and saluted. But the hall was strangely deserted, he noted half-consciously, even for the hour of the siesta. He frowned and told himself his supposedly loyal fascists were hiding this sultry July, with the low rumble in the hills surrounding indicating that thunder was on its way.

The major guarding his mistress's room snapped to attention, next to the chamberlain in his morning suit, who represented the court. "Good afternoon, Signor Mussolini," the latter intoned in that grave slow manner that all these courtiers affected.

Mussolini's heavy jaw dropped open with surprise for a moment. Why had the man greeted him like that? Why not 'Duce', as was customary? The man's horselike face revealed nothing but then the Italian leader told himself, all these pomaded, powdered *pederasti* were like that. He glanced at the young major with the Silver Cross for Gallantry on his chest. But his gaze was fixed on some distant horizon, as if he didn't want to meet the Duce's eyes.

"Duce," the voice came from behind the door and he dismissed the two of them immediately. It was Clara; she was waiting for him.

"You may go," Mussolini commanded icily, once again the man of destiny, leading his backward country to a great future, together with his comrade and ally, Adolf Hitler.

They went, but there was no zest in the way the young officer, who had won his medal for bravery in Libya and lost his left hand doing so, moved off. He, too, seemed to be affected by the heavy, broody staleness of the July day. He dismissed them from his mind. Whatever was going on, *they* would never enjoy the delights of the flesh that he would soon, not if they lived to be a hundred years old. Besides, he told himself, as Clara called, "Enter, beloved", what women would want another man, once she had been bedded by the 'Father of the Country', Benito Mussolini?

She lay sprawled seductively beneath the pale grey silken sheet. Underneath it, her nubile young body was outlined tauntingly. He could see those delightful contours – the sweep of the plump stomach, the thrilling roundness of her heavy breasts – in every last detail. It was a body, he told himself, made for love-making.

"Caro . . . caro mio!" she said in a husky voice, reaching up to greet him, the silken sheet slithering down to reveal her beautiful body.

He swept away her hand, almost angrily. On this strange July day, with the thunder beginning to rumble now quite clearly – the storm wasn't too far off – he was not in the mood for silly prattling and romantic foolishness. He wanted physical relief from the tensions he was being subjected to – and he wanted it quick.

Brutally, almost, he shoved her back on the bed. The sheet slithered to her knees. He licked suddenly parched lips and fumbled with his belt.

Five minutes later it was all over. Leaving Clara sprawled, body thrown carelessly on the rumpled sheet, he had changed his shirt, sprinkled himself with talcum powder and had dressed again. As the major and the palace flunkey appeared from the shadows yet again to take up their posts once more, he felt satisfied after Clara. All the same, that old feeling of unease had begun to creep back. *Why?* But there was no answer to that overwhelming question, as he clattered down the great staircase to the waiting Mercedes, yet another present from his great friend north of the Brenner Pass.

On the opposite side of the great Piazza, deserted save for the two swarthy little men sweating in their dark business suits, the car was waiting, engine already ticking over impatiently like a highly strung racing hound impatient to be let off the leash. Mussolini glanced at them. He didn't recognise them, but said to himself, "*Ovra*" – the Italian Secret Police. Obviously they had been placed there to guard him. The two noticed the look and raised their large-brimmed American-style hats politely. Mussolini touched his rimless black Fascist headgear in acknowledgement. His driver gunned his engine and then they were off, neatly turning out of the great square, the rumble of the storm ever closer now. It wouldn't be long before it broke over the Italian capital.

The bigger of the two civilians turned to the driver. "Get ready," he ordered. "Alfredo," he added for the benefit of the man crouched over the short-wave radio in the back of the car, "call in. Tell them *he's* on his way." He broke off suddenly. A small battered Fiat had nosed its way into the piazza and was following Mussolini's Mercedes slowly. "His gorillas," he announced, taking in the big man behind the wheel and the other, equally big, tense figure next to him. "Ex-cops," he concluded. "Dumb."

"Yes," his companion agreed, speaking out of the side of his mouth, as if he might be overheard, though the square was deserted. "Take 'em, as easy as falling off a log." He made a quick jerking movement with his right wrist. A knife slid down from within his jacket sleeve. Grinning evilly, he palmed it neatly and flicked open the long shining blade with one and the same movement. "They won't even know what hit 'em."

A moment later the third car was moving off, following the other two down the baking, deserted streets, as Mussolini approached ever closer to his date with destiny . . .

The major-domo stared out of the council chamber for a

Leo Kessler

moment. Outside it was as if a plague had struck the city, symbolising, he couldn't help thinking, the times to come. Down the Corso Umberto, the streets were empty. Still, they seemed to the black-clad servant, who moved about noiselessly on his rubber-soled shoes, oddly menacing. Perhaps it was the heat, he told himself. Although evening was already approaching, the temperature in Rome was still up in the mid-thirties. Carefully, with a snowy white handkerchief, he patted the beads of sweat from his high forehead. He sniffed. Here he was in the centre of the capital which smelled fragrantly of new-mown hay, as if they were in the middle of the *campagna*, stretching to the Alban Hills, brown and parched as far as the eye could see.

With an effort of will the major-domo dismissed the heat. He concentrated on the task at hand. He stared around at the long table at which the Grand Council would make its fateful decision. It was arranged like one of those grandiose parades that the members of Italy's ruling body had always loved in their heyday when all had been well with the state of Mussolini's 'New Romans'.

Twenty-eight ebony pen-rests, one for each member, and jotting pads, arranged on a polished horseshoe of expensive mahogany tables, which flanked the raised dais used by the speakers. At discreet intervals there were six desk lamps, which cast an amber glow on the room (for it was getting progressively darker; the storm would soon break) and illuminated the gold-framed masters by Veronese hanging on walls lined in royal-blue velvet. The major-domo gave a little tut-tutting sound. He was from Piedmont, where they didn't like such flamboyant opulence. The big council chamber was a little too showy for him. Somehow it didn't seem right to him that a day like this, when the history of Italy might well be changed,

10

could end with decisions being made against such a flashy background.

He shrugged. The main thing was that they got rid of the upstart so that the King could take over again and pull Italy out of this disastrous war at Hitler's side. Outside the thunder rumbled again and forked lightning split the grey lowering sky over the Alban Hills. It wouldn't be long now, the major-domo told himself.

The thought seemed to lend renewed speed and energy to his final actions. He flitted around the great table noiselessly, tugging and pushing, ensuring that everything was in its right place. Then finally he paused, wiped the opaque pearls of sweat from his brow once more and gazed at his handiwork for a moment. Then, satisfied, he clapped his hands and the great doors opened immediately to reveal the servants in their black knee breeches and bearing their silver platters as if they had been waiting behind it ready for his signal all the time.

He shushed them around the room, with their glasses and decanters, ensuring that the drinks were in the right place for the individual council members. "Water?" one of them paused and asked, as the sound of car engines rolling into the courtyard grew louder. "*Water?*" he repeated a little stupidly.

The major-domo frowned. Surely, after all these years, the servant should know where to place the carafe of iced water which the Duce usually drank on these occasions, while the rest of the grandees guzzled everything from English whisky to the homemade *grappa* of their native provinces. Then he understood. The servant with the carafe of water with the ice cubes floating in it knew. They all knew. This day the Duce might well not be here in this great sombre chamber to enjoy the water he affected as the leader of the 'New Romans'.

11

"Oh," he said a little angrily, "put it over there on that side table. We can get it for him if necessary." He waved his immaculately white-gloved hand in dismissal. Outside the car engines had stopped. There was the crunch of boots on the gravel. Greetings were exchanged. Someone started to say something very loudly – the major-domo thought it might be Grandi – then the voice sank to a whisper as its owner had suddenly become aware of the gravity of the situation.

Then there was silence, as the council members passed inside into the blessed coolness of Palazzo Venezia, broken only by the ominous rumble of the thunder getting ever closer.

It was five o'clock on the afternoon of Saturday, 24 July 1943, the day on which the future of Italy was going to be decided . . .

Chapter Two

The first drops of rain started to splatter down in the courtyard. They exploded with a hissing sound, as the hot tiles soaked up the moisture almost at once. But now the storm was directly overhead. The thunder was growing louder by the instant – drumroll after drumroll like that of a Wagnerian overture emphasising the drama of the events taking place inside the Palazzo Venezia.

The watchers in the shadows pulled up their collars as the rain started to beat down upon them. They could have sheltered in the car, they knew. But they knew, too, that they had to be on the outside, ready to move – and move quickly – once trouble started. Not the Duce's bodyguard. They had taken shelter in their car and the smaller of the two watchers in the shadows could see them smoking fitfully, their windscreen wipers going back and forth with an almost hypnotic regularity.

The violence of the storm increased, bringing colder air with it. After the stifling heat of the day, the watchers shivered, but not only with cold – there was fear and foreboding, too.

Inside the Palazzo, Mussolini, his face deathly pale, faced up to his accusers. One after another they had challenged his ability to continue ruling Italy. These men in their pompous, flashy black uniforms, all red sashes and sparkling medals, whom he had made – toadies to a man – in times past, were now turning against him. At first he had smiled contemptuously at their pathetic accusations – *he had ruined Italy by joining Germany . . . thousands of her young men had died in vain for the Nazi cause in Libya and Russia . . . in the ruined provinces they were starving . . . not only was there no coffee – there were no foreign assets to buy the beans – but no bread either . . . the peasants were down to eating 'bread' made of acorns and chestnuts . . .* But as the accusations mounted, thrown at him with a bitterness and vehemence that was almost frightening, his expression had begun to change. Slowly but surely Benito Mussolini began to realise that these 'old comrades' were after his life. Try as he could, he could not stop the shaking of his hands.

Outside the storm was now mounting to its full fury. The wind lashed the tall eighteenth-century windows making them rattle, the velvet curtains in front of them whipping back and forth as the candles – the power had already failed – flickered crazily.

Now it was Dino Grandi's turn to stand in the little box and face him with *his* accusations. He took his time like the poseur he was, Mussolini thought, stroking that dyed black beard of his. All the same Grandi, a hero of the trenches in the last war, was a man to be reckoned with. Of all those present this stormy evening, from general to judge, Grandi was the one with the most power *and* the ability to swing the others to his way of thinking.

In the same instant that the big bearded Italian opened his mouth to speak, the windows ceased rattling and the bitter lash of the raindrops on their panes seemed more subdued. It was as if Nature itself was impressed by Grandi. "Duce," he commenced, using the old title of leader when all the rest had refused to do so, as if he, Mussolini, had already been consigned to history and was no longer of any importance whatsoever. The old title made Mussolini's heart leap a little. Was Grandi going to come out on his side after all?

Mussolini was to be disappointed. "Duce," Grandi repeated. "You betrayed the Italian people the day you took up with the German – Adolf Hitler."

Mussolini opened his mouth to blurt out a retort, but thought better of it. He wouldn't give these toadies and turncoats the satisfaction of losing his temper in that startling, sometimes frightening manner of his. Talk was cheap; let them talk until he was ready to deal with them.

"Italy wasn't ready for this war," Grandi replied. "And you knew it. But in your overweening vanity, Duce, you joined Hitler against what has become a world coalition, with Russia and America now allied to England. It is a coalition that cannot be beaten." He paused as if he expected the Leader to say something, but again Mussolini remained silent, though now his brain was racing furiously. What were they up to, the Grand Council? Were they just going to reprimand him? Were they going to suggest that he broke off with Hitler, if that were possible, and make a separate peace with the Anglo-Americans – even they would not be prepared to talk with the Russians, their enemies of the last quarter of a century? He waited for Grandi to make his point or proposal, or whatever it was.

But when Grandi continued, he caught Mussolini by surprise, for he asked a question instead of making a ststement. "Duce," he said, "would you care to tell the Grand Council what your present relationships are with Churchill, the English Prime Minister?"

The question came out of the blue completely, catching the Duce totally off guard. For a moment or two he couldn't answer, as outside the terrible storm started to rage once more, making the members of the Council look at each other in awe, as if the elemental fury of this summer storm was somehow frightening and beyond man's understanding.

"*Churchill!*" he gasped finally. "What is this with Churchill? Haven't we been at war with England for three years now. Churchill . . . is . . . our worst enemy."

Grandi gave the suddenly ashenfaced Duce a sardonic smile, as if happy to have shaken him out of his unaccustomed silence at last. "My dear Duce, don't you think we know about your long-term correspondence with the Englishman? After all, we had our people in the Italian Legation in London, too, until war was declared. And," he lowered his somewhat dramatic actor's voice significantly, "we know that correspondence continued after war was declared between us and the English. You cannot deny it, Duce." He didn't wait for the Duce to bluster and deny the point. Instead, Grandi continued hastily, "We of the Grand Council take it that Mr Churchill has already made suggestions to you on how Italy can withdraw from this terrible war without incurring the wrath of the Führer. After all, there is a whole German Army, the Tenth, already on Italian territory, and it would not surprise us one bit if their Führer did not use that army to blackmail us into remaining at war with the Western Allies and Russia *if* he discovered in advance that we wish to make a separate peace."

Mussolini's head reeled. "Churchill . . . blackmail . . . a separate peace," he stuttered like some village yokel trying to comprehend events that were totally beyond his understanding.

Grandi raised an elegant hand with its manicured, lacquered nails to stop him. "Let us not waste time, Duce.

16

Let me tell you what the Grand Council has decided before you make your decision." He looked around the faces of the other members, as if for approval. One by one they nodded, some eagerly, as if they were glad to have made the decision and see it now in the open; others reluctantly, heads bent, still fearing, or so it seemed, the power of the Duce. Grandi clicked his fingers impatiently, as if in a hurry to get the matter over with. The council member seated next to him withdrew a paper hurriedly from his briefcase and handed it to the bearded Head of Council.

For once, Grandi didn't use his reading glasses and this time Mussolini knew it was not his vanity that made him do so. He knew the contents of the document by heart – he didn't need the glasses. He cleared his throat and began: "The Grand Council declares that to achieve the unity of the Italian people it is necessary to restore all functions back to the Crown immediately. For the honour and safety of the country, His Majesty the King should now assume effective command of all the armed forces." He paused. "That's all you need to know," he added brutally.

"But that means the end of fascism – *our movement!*" Mussolini said, aghast. "You can't—"

"There is an alternative, which might save you and the movement," Grandi said solemnly.

Mussolini grasped at straws. "What?" he asked desperately. "Please tell me. What can I do? I will do anything—" He never finished his desperate plea. As the thunder boomed right overhead, shaking the very room and threatening to extinguish the candles, the major-domo flung open the great doors and burst into the chamber. His Piedmontese calm had vanished. His face, streaked with raindrops, was contorted with fear and excitement. "Gentlemen . . . gentlemen!" he exclaimed. "We have just received word." He swallowed hard and tried to control his hectic breathing.

"Come on, man," Grandi urged angrily. "Word about what?"

"The Germans, Councillor . . . A company of Germans are on their way here. Our people have just spotted them."

"Heading here?"

"We think so."

Grandi's mind raced. He knew that Rome was full of spies – even the Russians had their agents in the capital, now that Italy had been invaded by the enemy – and there was need to raise the communist workers of the north in revolt. It was an ideal opportunity for the Russians to turn Italy into a communist state. Although the Germans were technically allies, they, too, had their agents spying on those Italians who ran the state. Perhaps the *tedeschi* had found out what was going on and were attempting to rescue the 'Führer's friend'? He didn't know, but he was taking no chances.

Outside, drenched by now, the raindrops dropping off their broad-brimmed hats, the three *Ovra* agents tensed. They could hear the sound of the heavy *Wehrmacht* truck quite plainly and they didn't need a crystal ball to know that the Germans were up to no good. Their leader flung a look at the Duce's car. The two big ex-cops were still inside – he could see them clearly outlined by the red light of the dashboard – but neither seemed to have noticed that something untoward was happening. Perhaps they were listening to headquarters over their short-wave radio. Whatever it was, the little *Ovra* man knew it was to their advantage. "*Allora*," he snapped, mind made up. He tugged out his pistol and wiped the muzzle against the dry inside of his sleeve. "Let's deal with them first."

The other two needed no urging. They didn't want to

get involved in a firefight with the *tedeschi*. Together they walked, crouched and alert, through the pouring rain, which was coming down in a white fury, their shoes squelching through the mud. Down the road the grinding noise of the German truck in low gear was getting ever louder. Now and again they could even see its blacked-out headlamps in gaps between the ornamental bushes.

In the car the two cops still did not move. The pelting rain was helping to drown any sound the killers' approach made. The little one paused and clicked off the safety catch on his long-barrelled pistol. The other two did the same. It wouldn't be long now before the cops heard them.

Already soaked, their clothes whipped around their skinny bodies. The killers were only twenty metres away when one of the cops started. Out of the side of his mouth, the leader hissed urgently, "The pigs have heard us." He raised his pistol, resting the long barrel on his left arm.

"Hey," the cop began, "what the h—" He didn't finish the question. *Phlat!* A soft plop. The cop yelped with sudden pain and went reeling back, his shattered face beginning already to slip to his chest like molten red sealing wax.

The man next to him recovered from the surprise attack remarkably quickly. He didn't hesitate. Instead he opened the door and fell out into the wet grass, dragging out his pistol from his shoulder holster as he did so. Next moment, crouched low and using the car's chassis as cover, he started running for the nearby bushes, firing as he went.

Scarlet flashes stabbed the darkness. The little *Ovra* man knew the running cop's shots weren't accurate, but he was stopping them moving forward and he daren't let him escape and raise the alarm. He stopped, controlled his breathing the best he could and, balancing the pistol on his left forearm, fired.

The running cop stumbled, caught himself and started to stagger on. In a moment he was going to disappear into the soaked, dripping bushes. But suddenly his luck ran out. The little man fired again. The slug slammed into the small of his back. The cop shrieked with pain and pitched face-forward, dead before he hit the grass.

Two metres away, the tall man crouched inside the bushes fought off the instinct to break cover and help the cop. He knew instinctively it would be to no avail. The cop was probably already dead or dying. So he remained where he was, hardly daring to breathe, watching the end of this violent drama which would change the course of the rest of the history of the Second World War.

With the German truck coming ever closer, the Italians acted swiftly. Hurriedly the Duce was hustled outside, a blanket thrown over his head to protect him from the storm, according to Grandi – in reality it was so that no one might recognise his uniform with the black-tassled cap of a field marshal. Out of nowhere a battered army ambulance rolled up. An army NCO threw open the rear door. Mussolini recoiled. The interior was like a furnace. It reeked of tar-disinfectant and faeces of the wounded it had transported earlier on. "God in heaven, not in that!"

Gently the NCO propelled him forward by his elbow. "Orders, *signor*," he said, in the soft accent of the South, "orders." Mussolini stumbled inside. Immediately other soldiers, all heavily armed, piled in after him. The Duce moaned and the watcher in the bushes had one last ludicrous cameo of the Italian leader's downfall. It would remain in his mind till he was very old, long after he had left Italy for good. It was of Mussolini with his cap askew, looking in horror at the sight of so many armed men crowding in after him. Next moment, with the grind of the German truck almost

20

upon them and with NCOs yelling out hoarse angry orders in their own harsh language, the ambulance had vanished into the storm.

The watcher hesitated. Then he told himself that the *tedeschi*, with their customary thoroughness, would search the whole area soon. It would be better not to be found by them. Tucking his collar around his neck against the driving rain, its drops racing down his face like bitter tears, the watcher limped away into the darkness. It was all over . . .

Chapter Three

All over a battered Berlin the sirens were beginning to sound the 'all clear'. One after another they began to take up the sound of relief, echoing and re-echoing down the great Ost-West Allee, from east to west as the Flying Fortresses departed. Here and there one of the great silver-painted bombers of the US Air Force was lagging behind the rest, closed up in their tight V patterns. Smoke trailed from crippled engines; some limped along scarcely above stalling speed, with huge sections of their fuselage shot away by the flak. And all the while the German fighters buzzed them frighteningly, zooming down and up, all about, impatient for the crippled planes to clear the city limits when they would shoot them out of the sky.

Not that anyone below cared about the *Amis*. They had been coming all week, day after day, while the Tommies had continued their deadly work of destruction at night. They had wreaked terrible destruction on the German capital, destroying whole areas of working-class suburbs close to the war factories. Even as he watched the departing enemy, the tall man, held up like the rest of the shabby crowd by an officious air-raid warden, could see the little man in his greasy bowler, shabby imitation leather briefcase held in his right hand, methodically kicking the dead body of a US airman sprawled on the debris-littered road, half enshrouded

22

in a bullet-riddled parachute that had failed to open. The little man's face showed no emotion, not even hatred. Perhaps, the tall man told himself, it was something the little Berliner thought he had to do to show the others that there was a need to take a revenge for this aerial savagery.

"Won't be long now," the middle-aged air-raid warden in his begrimed helmet said. "They're bringing out the rest of the animals now."

"Damn the animals," someone in the crowd snarled. "What about us?"

"You're animals as well," the warden replied without rancour. As four wardens from the shattered zoo urged on an elephant which was dragging a dead bloody giraffe through the debris, the tall man nodded to himself in agreement. He supposed they were animals – savage ones that killed with steel and fire instead of tooth and nail.

Behind the slow moving, solemn procession, there was a plump VAD nurse, tears running down her fat pale cheeks, a dead chimp cradled to her ample bosom. Every now and again she made little soothing noises like a fond mother might do to a frightened infant.

Hastily the tall man took his eyes off her and the dead monkey, with the dripping red stump where its little left leg had once been. He wasn't an emotional man by any means, but he was soldier enough to think that suffering belonged to the battlefield and not to these normally homely civilian surroundings.

Brakes squealed. The elephant started. In its fear it deposited a great steaming mountain of a turd near the giraffe's sightless head. One of the warders from the zoo cried angrily at the taxi which had slewed to a stop, the gas bag which powered the vehicle pulsating like a rubber lung on its roof. The driver popped out his head and yelled back,

23

"Who'd expect a giraffe and an elephant to be wandering about at this time o' day?"

"You want to be lacking a set o' teeth, friend?" the civilian cried threateningly.

The tall man, in his immaculate suit with the ribbon of the Iron Cross and the Italian *Croce d'Argento* in the button of the left side, didn't wait for the taxi driver's reply. Instead he called in a voice used to giving commands – and having them obeyed. "Taxi – Hotel Adlon. At once, please."

The mention of Berlin's top hotel did it. Even under these pretty terrible conditions, Berliners were still impressed by the name. After all even the Führer ate there sometimes. "*Jawohl . . . sofort, mein Herr,*" the taxi driver cried happily, eyes already seeing the fat tip and inflated fare he would receive from this obviously big animal.

A minute later the middle-aged taxi driver was weaving his way in and out of the debris littering the streets, paying no attention to the bodies sprawled out in the gutters in the extravagant postures of those done violently to death, as if he drove through a Berlin littered with corpses every day that dawned.

As always, the Adlon was an oasis of expensive calm. The porters, the bellboys and all the other servants who made life effortlessly easy for the rich, were in their accustomed places, brass buttons of their uniforms sparkling, faces revealing nothing of the brutal savagery of the night. High-ranking officers and civil servants mingled here and there with brown-uniformed Party bosses, all well-fed and blooming with health, moved in and out, saluting, bowing, shaking hands, exchanging compliments and news, as if the War were a thousand kilometres away and not on their own doorstep.

"*Tag,* Fritz," the tall man greeted the long-time commissionaire, all First World War medals, heavy belly and old-fashioned curved moustaches.

"*Guten Tag, Herr Legationsrat,*" Fritz replied, proud that he remembered the new arrival's title. It was part of his image never to forget the name of a guest; he spent his off-duty time mugging them up by year and name in the discreet little black book he kept in the tails of his frock coat.

The tall man passed inside. As usual a ladies' string quartet was scraping away in the lounge. When 'English Tea', as it was still called, was served at precisely four o'clock, they would break into what they thought was a spirited rendition of a Strauss waltz until finally, red-faced and panting, they would ask their listeners, if any, for "*eine kleine Pause*". The tall man grinned at the thought; nothing ever seemed to change at the Hotel Adlon.

He dismissed the quartet from his mind, concentrating on looking for Claudia von und zu Dodenburg, the woman he had come to meet on this last day of July. Over the phone the day before she had simpered in a conspiratorial manner that she had booked a 'double room' at the more discreet back of the hotel for the night. All the same, he wanted to get a few stiff drinks inside her before she went upstairs. She'd talk sooner that way. He knew that from past experience.

He glanced into the smoke-filled crowded bar. In his line of business, it was standard operating procedure. More often than not the people who might cause him problems would be drinking in the bar, eyes fixed on the ornate gilt-framed mirror behind it, watching the comings and goings in the elegant salon outside.

Without seeming to do so, he searched the place thoroughly, seemingly unable to make up his mind whether slip inside for a quick one before he got on with his business. He saw no one he knew until his gaze fell on the bar itself. Instantly he recognised the smallest of the four officers at the *Theke*. It was the 'Conqueror of Holland', as the Nazi Press had called him back in May 1940 when he had captured that country from the air virtually single-handed with his one parachute division. *General der Flieger* Student was chatting animatedly with a colonel, his broad face flushed and urgent, the scar on his forehead standing out an ugly red. Next to them a harshly handsome SS major, his skinny chest covered with battle decorations, listened without much obvious interest to what Student was saying. The tall man was about to dismiss them, when it struck him. All three of them were dressed in desert khaki. He frowned, puzzled. Why? he wondered. The Afrika Korps had been run out of the Western Desert in Africa these six months or more. So why were they wearing the special uniform?

But before he had more time to ponder the puzzle, an aristocratic voice to his rear said happily, "Ah, there you are, my dearest Fredo."

He turned, a little startled, though he recognised the voice at once, telling himself he had been living off his nerves too long; he had to get a grip on himself. Aloud he said, "How good of you to arrange everything, Claudia, especially with your busy schedule." He bent and pressed his lips to the back of her outstretched right hand. It smelt subtly of expensive French perfume.

She chuckled in her no-nonsense, hearty aristocratic fashion, her prettyish broad face set in a smile of pleasure. "No doubt I shall profit from the – er – arrangements, too, Fredo," she said and winked in a definitely unaristocratic fashion.

He smiled despite his tension. Claudia, a senior official in Himmler's Headquarters, was admittedly a tool of his, useful only so long as he needed the information she could supply. All the same she was a 'good sport', as he put it and in bed she wasn't too bad in a boisterous almost masculine fashion; the niceties of love-making were obviously lost on her.

Her smile increased as she put her arm through his possessively and snuggled her well-fleshed body closer to his, saying, "Shall we?" In the manner of the upper classes, she didn't believe in beating about the bush.

"Naturally, of course, *cara mia*," he replied hastily, lacing his answer with a couple of words of Italian; for he knew well how these dull plodding Germans loved what they regarded as the exotic flavour of the never-never land of the south, *bella Italia*. "But perhaps first a cocktail. It's been a hot day and an unpleasant one," he indicated the smoking rubble outside.

"Of course, of course, my poor dear," she said in an almost motherly fashion and squeezed his arm reassuringly. "You shall have your drink. We will both have one and *then* we shall get down to the other beautiful business," she lowered her voice significantly.

But that wasn't to be – just yet. At the bar, the harshly handsome SS Major with the cropped blond hair rose to his feet suddenly, a look of surprised recognition on his face. "Claudi," he called, "Claudia von Dodenburg."

Student and the Colonel frowned at themselves in the big bar mirror; then they saw the woman, dressed in the uniform of the 'SD', and their frowns turned to careful smiles as they bowed to her image in the glass.

With long strides the SS Major, who, as the tall man could see now, belonged to the elite SS Regiment 'Wotan', as the black and white armband proclaimed proudly, crossed the bar.

"Kuno," Claudia cried in delight, "my favourite cousin!"

Without ceremony the two cousins embraced and then, kissing her hand, Kuno von Dodenburg waited to be introduced to the middle-aged man with his sharp features and even sharper eyes, who looked more like a soldier than a civilian; he held himself in that way that only professional soldiers do.

"Fredo von Fallersheim und Ascona," Claudia said, as the two men shook hands, each trying to sum the other one up for reasons known only to themselves.

The tall man saw that although the SS officer was barely in his mid-twenties, he had the cagey, wary look of a man much older – one who had seen much tragedy and suffering. Kuno von Dodenburg, he decided instantly, was not a man to be trifled with. In the depths of those icy-blue eyes was the kind of arrogant ruthlessness that one only saw in men who had been pushed to the very limits of their endurance in battle. A little angrily he told himself it was a damned shame that Germany seemed to produce too many of such types, prepared, in the end, to throw away their precious young lives for 'Folk, Fatherland and Führer'.

"Fredo, here," Claudia was saying, while Kuno was still studying the tall Italian and deciding he didn't look one bit like the usual Italian – indeed with that haughty look and clipped, upswept military moustache, he seemed more an Englishman of the 'milord' type, "does something very hush-hush in the Italian Legation."

The tall man laughed easily and said in his perfect German, "Hush-hush? Oh yes – *hushing* to empty the ambassador's wastepaper basket." But even as he said the joking words, he realised that he had done so several times of late – ever since the trouble had started in Rome. The whole damned business had begun with startling suddenness.

"I see that—" von Dodenburg's question was interrupted

rudely by a a great raucous, drunken laugh, followed by the tinkle of broken glass and, a moment after that, one of those celebrated, long, not unmusical, extended farts well known throughout the SS NCO Corps.

Von Dodenburg's face blanched for a moment at the sound. Instinctively he knew it heralded trouble. Then he pulled himself together and touched his right hand to the rakishly tilted cap with the tarnished skull-and-crossbones and death's head insignia which had brought fear to half of conquered Europe. "Excuse me, von Fallersheim," he said hastily. "There has been a sudden emergency. Please excuse me, I must attend to it."

"Yes, yes," the tall man said, somewhat puzzled. Claudia placed a polite peck on her cousin's lean hard face and then he was gone, hurrying to the door of the great hotel, leaving the two of them to stare at his back in some bewilderment.

Finally they turned and, with the tall man guiding her, Claudia headed for the cocktail lounge, the Italian official limping slightly at her side, ignoring the discreet looks of the other patrons, who were obviously wondering what this civilian had to do with a female member of Himmler's dreaded 'Security Service'.

Chapter Four

"You might well be a general," Schulze was slurring, swaying dangerously as he faced up to the Adlon's elegant commissionaire. "But I'm from Wotan, get it?" He jerked a thumb like a hairy pork sausage at his chest, heavy with decorations won in campaigns in a dozen different countries and three different continents. "Sergeant Schulze of SS Assault Regiment Wotan and that about equals us up. Or else?" He thrust out his pugnacious jaw challengingly.

Squatting in a little wooden cart of the kind kids and old women used to collect firewood, Corporal Matz, his longtime running mate, wooden leg crooked over his shoulder, raised his head from a chamberpot full of beer and urged, "Go on, old house. Drop him in it. Who does he think he is, the ancient plush ears, to speak to an NCO of the Black Guards like that."

The exortation made no impression on a flushed, indignant Schulze, for he retorted, "Get yer snout out of them suds. Remember, half of 'em is mine." He turned to the harassed commissionaire once more. "Now then, you, are you gonna let me in to see my officer or not? If you waste any more o' my time, I'm gonna stick yer head so far up yer arse that yer glassy orbits will pop out of their frame!"

That terrible threat made the middle-aged commissionaire blanch. Still he stood his ground. "Now then," he said. "Be

30

reasonable. We can't have common NCOs in here, even if they are Wotan pavement pounders. The Adlon," he pronounced the revered name as if it were in quotes, "is reserved only for yer moneyed classes. What would *they* think if they were forced to hobnob with the likes of you, eh?"

Schulze snorted, "I had a bath last year. Well," he scratched the back of his shaven pate, as if making sure that he wasn't lousy, "I think it was last year. Anyhow, I ain't seen no felt lice on my alabaster torso since we came out of the line at Kursh and tidied up a bit. Soon got rid of the little buggers."

"Yer," said a happy drunken Matz, who wore a pair of silken knickers around his left sleeve as some kind of armband. "Yer even got that one that tried to dodge inter yer—"

"*Schulze . . . Matz!*" von Dodenburg's voice cut into their rambling harshly. "What's going on here? How did you manage to get into such bad order? We only managed to get off the troop transport four hours ago." He controlled his angry breathing with difficulty. "Anyway, what do you want me for?"

With great ceremony, Sergeant Schulze drew himself up and attempted to throw his CO a tremendous salute. He failed lamentably, so much so that he nearly fell into Matz's barrow, making him spill a little of the precious 'suds'.

"Hey!" he exclaimed. "Don't yer know that this," he clutched the chamberpot frantically, "is more precious than the milk of the Führer's wet nurse."

A passer-by glared at the little man for using the leader's name in that fashion. He opened his mouth to protest, but changed his mind immediately when he saw the look on Schulze's face.

"Enough of that," von Dodenburg snapped hastily. "Where's the fire, eh?"

"Two things, sir," Schulze said, suddenly embarrassed, twisting his head awkwardly, as if his collar were too tight for him.

"Go on, spit it out," von Dodenburg urged grimly.

"Sir," Schulze proclaimed solemnly, "it appears that we of Wotan are up to our hooters in the brown substance – to put it crudely, we're in the shit."

"How?" von Dodenburg demanded, trying to control his temper. For some reason he wasn't in the mood for Schulze's attempts at what he considered as humour.

"SS HQ Himmler called the CO an hour back. We're to be recalled, every man jack of us, even if we are in the gentle arms of our beloved." What looked like a single tear started to run down Matz's wizened, apelike face. In half a moment, it appeared, he might well break down and sob.

"Why?" von Dodenburg persisted.

"Because, sir, we're not staying at home here with Mother. We're off to the land where the spaghetti grows," Schulze answered simply; Matz began to sob.

Von Dodenburg threw up his hands, as if he were about go mad. Matz, drunk as he was, knew when he was overstepping the mark. His tears ceased immediately. Holding up the chipped white chamberpot, he enquired pleasantly, "Fancy a drink, sir? Good Munich suds." Von Dodenburg glared at him and he lowered the vessel at once, as if he had just been stung.

"*Italy?*" he demanded.

"Yessir," Schulze replied promptly. "To the land of the *signoras* with—"

"Shut up," von Dodenburg interrupted him. "I can't hear myself think." Rapidly he considered the information. It tied in with Student's tropical uniform and what the General had hinted about his parachute division, the 'Green Devils', as he called them proudly. The *Wehrmacht* High Command was moving large numbers of troops into Italy at a moment's notice and it was pretty obvious it had to do something with the sacking of Mussolini. What exactly, he didn't know or care. Indeed at that moment, despite the smoking ruins, death and destruction all around him, he felt happy suddenly. They weren't going back to that accursed Popovland again. Anything was better than Russia! "How long have we got before recall?" he asked finally.

Schulze's eyes twinkled roguishly. "Well, enough, sir." He gave a mock sigh. "Though I do think I'm going impotent. I've only cocked my leg over twice already this morning."

"*When?*"

"Twenty hundred hours this night, sir," Schulze answered promptly. "Time enough to dance the mattress polka with some willing pavement pounder at least." He gave a sigh.

"Be off with you," said von Dodenburg curtly, with a wave of his hand, "and remember to be there in time, both of you. Thanks for telling me."

Matz took another huge drink of his 'suds', beer foam all around his lips, and chortled. "All right, coachman. Let us be on our way tootsweet. I shall probably get engaged this night. There is not a moment to waste."

Schulze mumbled something unprintable under his breath then, seizing the wooden handles of the homemade kid's cart, started to push his old comrade, guzzling beer all the while, back the way they had come.

Standing next to the door the shabby old woman who sold little bouquets to the Adlon's guests wiped away a tear with her gnarled knuckles, quavering, "What brave boys,

our soldiers. The things they must have been through, sir."
She wiped away another tear.

"Yes, the things they must have been *through*," von
Dodenburg echoed. Then under his breath he added a little
maliciously, "And no doubt they'll have been through a few
more before this day is out . . ." With that he turned and
started to stroll leisurely in the same direction that the two
NCOs had taken, his brow wrinkled in thought.

Behind him, the two lovers rose from their table, ignoring
the noise their shoes made on the broken glass from the
raid the night before. For once the Adlon's famous service
had slipped up. Together they threaded their way out of
the now crowded cocktail bar, both grateful that it was
crowded. No one took any notice of them, and each for
his own reasons didn't want to be noticed, especially in
this particular scandal shop.

An hour later, sweaty and tired, they rested in the big rumpled bed, smoking fitfully and bathed in a blood-red light, for
she had placed a pair of red silk knickers over her bedside
lamp to subdue the glare. "More romantic that way," she had
said, as she had stripped naked. He had nodded his agreement, though the tipsy German aristocrat was one of the least
romantic women he had ever bedded. Like German food, her
love-making was solid and satisfying, but without the least
kind of sophistication. Still, as he told himself, listening to
the sounds of the German capital settling down for the night
and the usual RAF bombing raid, she served her purpose.
Besides, he wasn't chancing his neck with a high-ranking
female member of Himmler's feared security service for the
sophistication she could bring to their rutting. He breathed
out a stream of blue smoke. Outside a hoarse official voice
was crying, "Will you turn that light out up there. It's already
dark, you know. Or do you need glasses?"

"Penny for them?" she asked and gently ran her big hand, hardened by years of reining in thoroughbreds, down the side of his handsome tanned face.

He hesitated, though he had rehearsed his method approach many times over the last forty-eight hours. "I've got bad news – of a kind," he added hastily as he felt her start with shock.

She raised herself and looked down at him.

"Not that bad," he calmed her. "Might well be that I shall be sent back to Rome. You know why."

She took the bait without hesitation. "Mussolini?"

He let her wait before he said simply, as if it wasn't very important really. "Yes, the Duce."

"We have plans," she said after a while.

Again he took his time. Outside the air-raid wardens were checking the tickets for places in the great overhead air-raid shelter, which could sway up to nine degrees if a bomb landed close by, without collapsing.

"What kind of plans?" he asked finally, forgotting the noise outside.

"The Führer has ordered that we must give all the aid we can to his old comrade—"

"Military aid?" he cut in quickly.

"Yes." She looked at him strangely. Hastily he pressed his hand deeper into the damp warmness between her legs. She gave a sigh of pleasure, any suspicions she might have had vanishing quickly. "But also other help, too."

"How?"

"*Reichsführer* SS Himmler is putting a team together to find the Duce. The plans are already completed as far as I know. *Hm,*" she sighed. "That's nice." Her bosom began to rise and fall hectically. He tried one more thing. To do more, especially now, would undoubtedly arouse her suspicion;

she wasn't *that* foolish, even when she was in the throes of passion. "Who's in charge of the team? I'd like to report it to the Ambassador. It might set him at ease."

"Skorzeny," she answered dreamily, totally wrapped up in her own sexual pleasure. Suddenly her face flushed an ugly, even, angry red. "Oh, come on . . . *do it to me – quick!*" She might have been back on her father's estate in East Prussia, supervising the insemination of an eager cow by one of the farm's more reluctant stud bulls. He didn't mind. Now he had a name. Swiftly he thrust her legs further apart and thrust himself inside her.

Skorzeny was the last thing he could remember thinking.

Chapter Five

It was hardly a dinner to grace the table of a hero and a full General to boot, but *General der Flieger* Kurt Student, jovial and crop-headed, ate with relish. There were three of them eating at the little card table, attended to by a single soldier, who didn't even have a white mess jacket, but served them in his shirt sleeves. "Good honest German fare," Student proclaimed, swallowing another half a gherkin with the pork and black bread. "Can't beat it." He reached out for the little glass of ice-cold *Schlichte*, cried, "*Prost, meine Herren*," and downed the fiery schnapps in one gulp. Almost immediately he followed it with a sip of his beer. "*Lütt un' Lütt* they called it where I come from," he explained to the other two who were toying with their food. "Little and little. Ideal for washing fat pork belly down yer gullet. *Ha-ha!*"

The others didn't join in the General's hearty laughter.

Student was not a sensitive man, but somehow he guessed the other two were not particularly impressed by his evening meal, yet the knowledge didn't worry him. He was a General, a favourite of the Führer himself. They were just field grade officers of little importance, though the CO of SS Assault Regiment Wotan, nicknamed the 'Vulture' on account of his monstrous beak of a nose sitting opposite him, was the darling of the Waffen SS. The other man, a huge Austrian with a scarred face like the work of a butcher's apprentice gone crazy, was a complete stranger to him.

Otto Skorzeny, as the SS Major was called, had told them only moments before that he had been called to attend the Führer that very day – for reasons that had not been explained to him at the time. A little later he had found himself with six other young officers from both the SS and the *Wehrmacht* facing Adolf Hitler personally. In turn they had been introduced to the Leader, who had asked each whether he knew Italian or Italy. All had answered in the negative except he, Skorzeny, who had told the Führer that he had toured Italy twice before on his motorbike.

The Führer had paused then and had asked, "Well, Skorzeny, what do you think of the Italians?"

The giant SS man hadn't hesitated, though he guessed his answer might offend Hitler. Straight off, he had barked, "*Mein Führer*, I am an Austrian like yourself. What can an Austrian think of a country, even an allied one, that stole one of its provinces, the South Tyrol, from it after Austria's defeat in 1918?"

That had done it. "I thought the Führer was going to fall over me, gentlemen," he had explained to the other two. "But he clapped me on the shoulder, told me to wait till he dimissed the others." The scar-faced giant savoured the moment while the Vulture stroked that monstrous beak of his and told himself that the big man was a typical Austrian – all charm and selfishness. Still, if whatever the Führer had planned for him and SS Assault Regiment Wotan brought him to those general's stars, which he craved as much as he did the exciting naked bodies of teenage youths, he could even tolerate the 'comrade of the laced boot' opposite him.

After Student, mouth full of meat and bread, had urged

him to "Get on with it, Major," Skorzeny had related how the Führer had told him about the arrest and disappearance of the Italian dictator, Mussolini, thirty-six hours before. Now he wanted Skorzeny to find him so that a rescue attempt could be executed to free his 'old comrade in arms.' "Then, gentlemen," the Austrian had concluded, hardly able to conceal his pride and self-importance, "the Führer gave me carte blanche. All doors are to be opened to me. The rescue of the Duce has priority number one." He had beamed at the other two with his terribly scarred face.

Student frowned. "*All?*" He had echoed, suddenly angry. "My dear Skorzeny, you can't go around commanding – er – full generals."

The Vulture grinned to himself. The 'full general' in question was obviously Student himself.

Skorzeny hadn't risen to the bait. Instead he had quietly tapped the left breast pocket of his tunic, as if to signify that the document it contained was all he needed – it would open all doors.

The spartan meal finished, Student drained his beer, belched like a good 'front swine' should to signify that he had enjoyed his 'fodder', as the men in the line called their rations, and said, "All right, gentlemen, let us look at the situation."

"Please," Skorzeny said, and even as he sat there he bowed slightly from the waist. Like a damned greasy Austrian waiter in a coffee house, the Vulture said to himself, but his ugly face revealed nothing of his contempt.

"Presently there are eight armoured divisions of the *Wehrmacht* in Italy," Student explained. "But they will be employed in dealing with the Allies, once the Anglo-Americans start to invade the Italian mainland which they will undoubtedly do soon." He let the information sink in before continuing with, "The Führer has, however, given me three divisions in the form of an Airborne Corps for 'internal security purposes'."

The Vulture couldn't resist the opportunity that the announcement gave him. He screwed his monocle more firmly in his left eye and rasped in his hard Prussian fashion, "Aha, we're going to shoot some macaroni, eh?" He grinned, displaying a mouthful of gold teeth.

Kurt Student frowned severely. "Not exactly. We're in trouble enough in Italy. We don't want to rouse the population against us. No, it is intended that the Corps should take over key points, especially in Rome, and restore calm until we discover the location of Mussolini's prison. *Then* – and only *then* – will we use men of that Corps against the Italians – if necessary."

Hastily Skorzeny butted in: "The Führer told me that neither the German Commander-in-Chief in Italy nor our ambassador must know of this business. He said *they* would tackle the job in totally the wrong way."

The other two officers looked at him but said nothing. Skorzeny understood. His sallow scarface flushed angrily.

Student continued as if the Austrian hadn't spoken and the Vulture told himself that there was already bad blood between this young upstart and the veteran soldier who had earned his wings in the First World War. "So, in essence we are prepared for most eventualities. We can drop from the air. Thanks to you, Colonel Geier, we have one of the best armoured regiments in the whole of the Greater German Army—"

"*The* best," the Vulture corrected him, but Student wasn't listening. He looked at Skorzeny, a look that was lost on the Austrian. "So if Intelligence does make a mess of things – which it mostly does, I must point out – we are ready for immediate business. Now the code word for all units involved," he lowered his voice, as if he half suspected someone might be listening at the door, "is '*The macaroni's burning*'."

"How apt," the Vulture commented with a sardonic smile.

Student ignored the comment. Instead, he said, "Skorzeny, report."

For a moment the big Austrian looked bewildered, then he gathered what was expected of him. "Twenty picked men are going with me, all Italian speakers. We will be given civilian suits, weapons and silenced revolvers, laughing gas, tear gas and smoke grenades, plus thirty kilos of plastic explosive – and a stock of British five-pound notes, forged in the concentration camps." Student nodded his approval and in a small voice Skorzeny then added the final item, as if he was already well aware it was going to cause ridicule. "And – er," he looked down at his hands, "two complete outfits for Jesuit priests."

"What did you say?" Student snapped.

Skorzeny repeated the statement and the Vulture sniggered aloud. "What do you intend, Skorzeny? To preach them a sermon or something?"

Skorzeny, looking a little crestfallen for the first time since the impromptu briefing commenced, said nothing. "All right," Student interrupted urgently. "Let's not waste any more time. With the Führer breathing down our necks, every minute counts. You, Geier, will leave with your tanks and panzer grenadiers at midnight – the fewer who see you depart the better."

Colonel Geier nodded his understanding.

"Your people – including the Jesuits . . ." Student couldn't resist the dig – Skorzeny looked unhappy and wished he

41

had never mentioned the Jesuit outfits – ". . . will fly with me and my Corps staff at dawn tomorrow. My brave green devils will follow by road. As soon as we reach Rome we shall begin the operation." He paused for breath, his face brick-red with the effort. "And let us get this straight from the start: I am in overall command. I make the decisions, although you have carte blanche from the Führer himself, Skorzeny." He looked at the Austrian as if he were seeing him for the very first time. "The division of labour is simple, gentlemen. You, Skorzeny, find the Duce. I – and Colonel Geier – will rescue him. Is that clear?"

"*Einverstanden,*" the Austrian agreed quickly enough, but there was no enthusiasm about the reply, Geier told himself. Skorzeny had plans of his own, whatever they were, and they did not include *General der Flieger* Student.

The latter gave them a fake little smile and clicked his fingers. As if he had been hiding behind the door all along, waiting for this signal, the orderly appeared, bearing a tray with a fresh bottle of *Schlichte* and three glasses.

Hurriedly the orderly poured out the fiery alcohol and passed each of the three officers a glass. Student raised the glass level with the third button of his tunic, as Army Regulations prescribed. The others did the same. Student intoned, "I give you a toast, *meine Herren.* To the speedy and successful rescue of the Italian Duce."

"To the speedy and successful rescue of the Italian Duce."

"*Prost – ex*" Student barked and downed the contents of the glass in one gulp. Next moment he had thrown the glass at the wall, where it shattered at once, making the orderly start a little. The other two glasses followed and for a moment the three of them simply sat there like actors frozen into a tableau before the final curtain of a fifth-rate play.

The decision had been made. The hunt for Benito Mussolini had commenced!

Mr Yates and Colonel Pitman

The Rolls he had sent to pick him up at Liège started to slow down, something for which Yates was glad. The local driver had gone like a bat out of hell for the last eighty kilometres, traversing the frighteningly steep Ardennes hills and narrow cobbled roads as if they were not there, ignoring the Belgian cops' speed traps and barreling through the one-horse villages of the area, scattering the slow-witted peasants, as if the fifty kilometre speed limit didn't exist.

Obviously they were about to reach their destination, for as far as Yates could make out from the map of the border area balanced on his knees they were very close to the German frontier; and his destination was still inside Belgium. "Sind wir bald da?" he asked in German and then repeated the question in French, for around here the people were bilingual. But all he got for his pains was a few words grunted in a language he couldn't understand; he took it to be a local patois.

The Roll slowed down even more. Up ahead he could see the turrets and spires which the Belgian nouveaux riches *had built for themselves in mock Gothic styles back in the late nineteenth century, when they had established their* manoirs *to escape the industrial grime of Liège. They turned into a drive. Gravel crunched under the Rolls's tyres. They passed well-tended gardens and a summer house which was as big as the average worker's flat. Mentally Yates noted the fact. He might use the details when he came to write the series, depending upon what he thought of the Englishman he had come to see.*

Yates noted, too, that there was something vaguely sinister about the chateau. He couldn't quite figure out why, but

*there was. Was it the absence of people or the fact this
area had seen some of the bloodiest battles of the Second
World War – to the right of the house itself there were
the old shellholes, patched up now, of course, where the
stables had been clobbered by some long-forgotten artillery
barrage.*

*The Rolls squeaked to a stop. A servant in a green baize
apron stepped from the shadows. Obviously he was going
to help the chauffeur with Yates's baggage, though there
wasn't much of it. Beyond through the open door, he
glimpsed a maid in a short apron, busy dusting. She looked,
at a distance, quite pretty.*

*"Par ici, m'sieur," the servant in the green baize apron
said and extended his hand to indicate the direction Yates
should take.*

*Yates followed. He was impressed by the place. But
'veteran newshound', as he always thought of himself, in
that antiquated Fleet Street phrase – his colleagues on
the* Telegraph *would have laughed him out of the office if
they had known – that he was, he didn't show that he was
impressed. Indeed, to show that he had seen it all before,
he kept his hat on at its usual jaunty angle.*

*Their footsteps clattered over the decorative tiles through
the sombre cheerless furniture. Massive mahogany side-
boards and bent, glass-fronted cupboards groaned under
the weight of forgotten pots and glassware. Everything was
probably Meissen or Waterford. Still he wasn't impressed.*

*The two of them started to mount the great creaking
staircase flanked with dusty suits of armour on both sides,
with, in the gallery, faded fringed flags from forgotten
conflicts hanging above them.*

*A pretty maid was up there, too, dusting the portraits on
the wall, standing on tiptoe on a chair to reach them with*

her feather duster so that he could see her shapely thighs and trim bottom. "Worth a sin or two," he said to himself with a sardonic smile, living up to his supposed reputation as a hard-drinking, wenching newspaper man.

The girl, although she had her back to him, seemed to sense that he was looking up her skirt and she waggled her pert buttocks. Yates swallowed hard. The old man had invited him to spend the night and old men usually went to bed early. Perhaps – but he didn't finish that exciting thought for now the servant in the green baize apron said in German this time, "Ihr Zimmer, mein Herr." He allowed Yates to pass by – the servant seemed as old and as musty as the chateau's furniture – into the huge bedroom.

An ancient sagging bed dominated the room. Next to it there were the usual continental night tables of yore, probably with two pisspots, too, Yates told himself, and a few faded portraits and paintings on the walls. There was nothing about it to indicate that its owner was an Englishman – or was he? – save for a yellowing photograph on the wall to the left. He crossed to it and looked at the half-a-dozen men and a dark-haired woman in battledress, holding a Sten gun. There was something written beneath in Italian, he thought, but one thing was clear. The men were Englishmen, and it wasn't just the uniform which marked them as such – it was their faces, English faces of a kind that had long disappeared, square and self-confident, looking out at the world and radiating the belief that as long as you were English, you were all right. Let the foreigners make a muck-up of things; the English never would – or could.

"Which one is the Colonel?" Yates asked when he saw the servant was watching keenly.

"On the picture?" the man asked somewhat stupidly, or so Yates thought.

The Englishman nodded.

The servant shrugged. "I don't know, sir. The Colonel never speaks about the War."

Yates frowned. A picture from those days would have been very useful, but before he could pursue the subject the servant said, "The girl will help you to unpack, sir. Anything you need for the time being, please ring your bell. The Colonel expects you for dinner at eight o'clock – sharp." Even in German, which Yates had some difficulty understanding, that 'punktlich' came through clearly.

Yates waited till the servant had gone, then he crossed over again to the photograph of the bronzed, happy young men of another time. He stared at it intently, as if he were trying to read something into it. Obviously, he told himself after a while, it had been taken in wartime somewhere in the Med. The bronzed arms, the shirt sleeves rolled up, the men squinting slightly as if peering into a very bright sun, and above all the girl with the dark hair and the Sten gun – a partisan possibly. He pursed his lips. All that and the Italian inscription fitted into what he had already learned in his researches in London. But thousands – hundreds of thousands – of British troops had served in the Second World War in the Med. These officers didn't seem any different from what he would expect from crude amateur photos of that time over half a century ago.

"Bugger it," he cursed under his breath and in the same instant the pretty maid in the short skirt knocked at the door, eyed him coquettishly and got about her work, reaching very dangerously across the big bed every time she took out one of his things. Then all thoughts of that ancient war and the puzzle were forgotten . . .

*   *   *

49

Colonel Pitman, huddled in a rug as well as a thick winter-weight suit, although it was mid-autumn, stared out of the French window at Germany. The dinner had been frugal – "Carbonnade," the Colonel had explained. "Beef cooked in beer. Meat falls apart in your mouth. Good when you're old and wonky." But there had been plenty of wine and the Colonel had kept sipping, as if it were some kind of medicine, from the cut-glass tumbler of whisky at his elbow. Every time his wizened old face flushed red for a moment before growing grey and dead once more. Watching him in one of the silences the Colonel was given to, Yates characterised him as a 'grey man in a grey suit in a grey time.' He liked the phrase. He'd whip it down in his laptop as soon as he got upstairs again before the maid came, as she had half promised to do.

"A funny area," the Colonel wheezed, breaking the heavy brooding silence again. "Border areas always are." He coughed and his skinny, frail body trembled alarmingly. He looked as if he might fall apart at any moment. With a claw, covered with liver spots, he reached for his tumbler of whisky and took a shaky sip of the Scotch.

Yates frowned with distaste. He always disliked interviewing old people. It seemed they always lived for their illnesses one way or another. Either they talked interminably about their affliction or it got in the way of conversation, with coughs, sneezes, gasps for breath, the taking of pills to relieve symptoms. For Yates, old men were always a constant reminder of his own mortality. The time had come, he told himself, watching with distaste as the Colonel spat, his mouth covered by his skinny hand, into a jar of opaque liquid from his clogged-up lungs on the table next to the whisky.

"Sorry, Yates," he gasped, his lungs wheezing audibly, "one of the pleasures of old age. Where was I now?"

Yates, his drinker's face set and determined, was not going to let the old man go back to the peculiarities of the border area, whatever they were. He snapped, "Colonel, you have been very kind to receive me like this and put me up at very short notice, when you're obviously not too well."

The Colonel waved his hand vaguely, as if to dismiss the point and croaked, "Pleasure of your company is welcome. Sick of talking to the locals. Their dialect is abominable. Now," his voice rose with an effort of will on his part, as if he were making a physical effort to drag himself away from this remote border country into the world that his visitor had just come from. "Your editor referred me to 'Sambo', er, Lieutenant General Keene, who gave you and your paper a clean bill of health. So that's why I agreed to speak to you." The old man attempted a smile and his yellow, ill-fitting false teeth slid to the side of the wrinkled mouth – for one dreadful moment, Yates thought they were going to fall out altogether. They didn't and the Colonel continued, "Though God knows why you want to speak to old crocks like me." He looked at Yates and somehow the latter had a feeling that the 'old crock' was not as senile as he tried to make out he was. "I gather, however, it is something to do with the time I spent in the Army."

Yates felt himself going a little red with embarrassment. That was the ploy he had agreed upon with the editor to gain the old General's confidence so that he would recommend him to Colonel Pitman, who was proving a very hard man to find. He'd not even attended the Cavalry Club for years.

"Yessir," Yates said somewhat reluctantly, knowing that he had reached the point of no return. He had to chose his words carefully. He didn't want the old boy to clam up on him by asking his first questions in the wrong maner. These

51

upper-crust old boys could be nasty buggers if you rubbed them up the wrong way. "In a way."

"In a way. What way?"

Yates took the bull by the horns. He knew he'd have to come round to the post-war business eventually. "Your wartime experiences might play a role somewhere along the line – I don't know at the present . . ."

Colonel Pitman gave a little wintry smile at the other man's obvious discomforture. As old and as feeble as he was, he had clearly struck a senitive point. But he said nothing.

"But at the moment I'm concerned with what you might know, as one of our post-war military attachés to our embassy in Rome, in relation to . . ." he glanced down at the name inked on his left palm – newshounds never carried papers – it looked too amateurish . . . "a certain German soldier, one Otto Skorzeny, if I've pronounced the name correctly?"

"You have, young man," the Colonel croaked, obviously enjoying the discomfiture of his visitor from London.

"You've heard of him, sir?"

"Yes, of course. Everyone still surviving from my generation has. After all, it isn't every day that a German whom Eisenhower – he was the American commander of Allied forces in Europe in the War – called 'Public Enemy Number One' is praised publicly by a British PM in Parliament, what?"

At any other time, Yates would have laughed out loud at that use of 'what'; in itself it amounted virtually to a caricature. But not now.

"Yes," the Colonel continued, sitting up a little and peering down the winding hill road that led to the German border. "Fifty-odd years ago he came up that very road to carry out his tricks in the Battle of the Bulge."

"Who, sir?" *Yates was suddenly puzzled.*

"Skorzeny, of course."

Abruptly Yates realised they weren't just talking about people in books and newspapers. No, they were discussing men who'd loved, fought and died. He took the plunge. "I believe that when you were military attaché in Rome in the early fifties, you had occasion to meet Skorzeny – er, in Milan."

"No, in Venice, to be exact," Colonel Pitman corrected him gently and then looked Yates directly in the face. Admittedly the Colonel's eyes were the faded, rheumy ones of an old man, but there was a sudden hard keenness in them, too, which was definitely not that of a man well into his seventies.

Yates took time to recover. He had never thought, as he had mulled over the situation in the plane from Heathrow to the little airport just outside Liège, that he would have gotten Colonel Pitman to talk so swiftly. But here he was, almost admitting that he knew about Skorzeny and that in some function he had been present at that fateful meeting in Venice in the fifties – the meeting which had brought him to this remote place in the first place.

"I took a great deal of time finding you, Colonel," he stuttered, while he absorbed the information. "The Ministry of Defence was of no use. Neither was the Cabinet Office. From what little I did gather, people thought that you were already long dead." He hesitated and then added hastily, "Though, I, for one, am glad that you aren't."

Pitman looked at him. "Are you now?" he said in that crusty way of the English upper classes. "Yes, I suppose you are, being a journalist." Then it came out, very reasonably, very quietly, almost in a matter-of-fact tone. "It's Churchill, isn't it?" It wasn't a question, but a statement of fact. "The

53

Churchill Papers *to be exact . . ." With a little sigh, the skinny old man leaned back in his stiff, high-backed chair, his wizened face almost hidden in the growing gloom of the big room, and waited for it to happen . . .*

Part Two

THE SEARCH

Chapter Six

The big man in the faded blue uniform of the *Kriegsmarine* staggered up from the coastal road that led to the villa on the outskirts of the port. Under his arm he clutched a bundle of washing tied up in a towel. To any one of the barefoot, fat, native women and the fishermen in their patched overalls who might be watching him as he swayed back and forth, talking to himself as usual when he was drunk – which was most of the time – he was heading for the laundress's cottage, high on a hill above the Villa Weber. But in the fierce mid-morning heat no one on the sleepy little naval base of La Maddalena Island, just off the northernmost tip of Sardinia, took any notice of the giant drunk. He was an ordinary sailor, who spent most of his free time going from one dingy waterfront bar to another, downing the cheap local *grappa* and *vino* to get drunk. How he managed his duties in that state, in the gleaming white E-boat anchored in the little harbour under the fluttering white flag of the German Navy was anyone's business; but in this last week of August 1943 no one was interested in the *tedeschi* and their affairs save when were they going, now that the Duce had vanished and it was obvious that soon, very soon, Italy would be leaving the War as Germany's ally.

Skorzeny, hot, sweaty, his stomach doing backflips due to the rich, greasy food of the waterfront bars, cursed as he staggered up the burning white road that led to the cottage. Not only did he feel hot and ill, but also something of a fool in the undersized uniform lent to him by the skipper of the E-boat. Still, he knew the pretext had to be kept up if they were to rescue the missing Italian dictator.

The last twenty-nine days since he had left General Student and Colonel Geier at Rome Airport had been very frustrating. They had received lead after lead, but all had turned out fruitless. For days on end it had been one long wild-goose chase. Even when they managed to get on the missing Mussolini's trail, his Italian captors had been one jump ahead of the Germans and had spirited their prisoner away just before they had been about to strike. "*Zum Kotzen!*" he had cursed more than once and he had been right. It had all been very sick-making.

Then luck had turned in their favour. The German secret service had picked up a call from the Italian Admiral in charge of Anzio some 250 kilometres away to install a direct line between his office and a house – the Villa Weber – on the remote island of La Maddalena. It had not taken long for Skorzeny and his harassed searchers to figure out why. The Admiral was in charge of that whole sea area and would be the ideal link between Rome, through Anzio, to the remote island, cut off from the mainland save by boats of the Italian Navy. Naturally these craft could be not be stopped and searched for they were still, in theory at least, allies of the German *Kriegsmarine*.

Swiftly a plan had been worked out. It had been approved by Hitler personally, and Skorzeny, to his delight, was to play a major role in it. At six o'clock on the morning of 28 August, German craft carrying SS commandos would make a dash for La Maddalena, where they would join the six E-boats already there on a 'courtesy visit'. On the following morning the whole fleet would set sail on a training exercise. But once out of the harbour, the commandos would land and storm Villa Weber under covering fire from the ships. Immediately thereafter they would dash for Anzio from whence Mussolini would be flown to Rome and finally delivered into the Führer's safe keeping.

Some of the rescue party had doubted that the Duce was actually in the Villa Weber, but a drunken commando who spoke fluent Italian had ventured up to the mountain-top house where he had spotted Mussolini only metres away, sitting on an upright wooden chair, staring vacantly at the sea.

The layout of the Villa Weber, hidden by high walls, remained unknown to the attackers; and it was for this reason that Skorzeny, clad as an ordinary seaman, was on his way to the washerwoman this day in order to find out more about the defences and the layout. The washerwoman's cottage overlooked the villa and gave a good view of the ground floor which was the key to the success of the surprise attack soon to come.

Now moaning and clutching his stomach with his free hand, as if he were in acute pain, Skorzeny dumped his washing on the washerwoman's table and groaned in his broken Italian, "*Mama mia* – such pain!" He pointed to his yellow-stained underpants. "Dysentery," he explained – the word was almost the same in Italian. "I feel my insides are ruined." He groaned miserably yet again. "*Gabinetto, per favore.*"

The fat Italian woman with the worn features and grey hair shook her head, "*Niente.*"

Humbly she explained she hadn't got a toilet. It was what Skorzeny had expected. "*Fuori?*" he said hastily, as if he couldn't contain himself much longer, grabbing at his bell-bottoms, "*Si . . . si?*"

"*Si,*" she replied.

The giant didn't wait for further instructions. He dashed outside, and clambered up a rockside so that he could see the Villa Weber but was out of the sight of the washerwoman in her pathetically poor kitchen.

He crouched and ripped down the navy blue trousers for realism. The place had obviously been owned by someone of wealth or importance. The garden was well tended. The walls bristled with terracotta lions and eagles and was broken by vivid splashes of colour from the bougainvillea. But the watcher had no eyes for beauty. Instead he searched the place and especially the terrace for any signs of the missing man – and he knew now that the Duce had to be there. There were at least twenty heavily armed *carabinieri* guarding the the villa!

But there was no sign of Mussolini. Skorzeny wondered why he wasn't even allowed to sit on his own terrace in the Italian fashion during the hot period of the day. He pulled up his trousers and made a show of wiping his bottom on a copy of the Führer's own newspaper, *Der Volkische Beobachter* and then hastened back to the cottage. He had seen enough of the ground floor and the numbers and positions of the guards to be able to brief the assault party. Now suddenly very sober, he started walking back down the hill, his pains abruptly forgotten, munching a bunch of grapes sold to him by the elderly washerwoman.

Halfway down he fell in with a body of carabinieri obviously going on duty. Skorzeny began to chat with them, offering them grapes and praise of all things Italian. "*Bella Paese . . . ragazzi . . . vino . . .*" and the like. The cops were pleased. They beamed up at the German giant with his crazy Italian. Casually, Skorzeny broke off and said with sudden seriousness, "It was such a pity about the

Duce. This morning *Deutschland Funk* reported that your beloved Mussolini is dead."

The biggest carabiniere shook his head. *"Impossible, signor . . . impossible . . ."* he pronounced with an air of finality.

"But it's true," Skorzeny objected. "I had all the details of his complaints from a German doctor I know."

Again the big cop shook his head. "No," he said, *"il Duce* still lives. I must know you know." He turned and grinned at his comrades, as if to say: Are these *tedeschi* wooden-headed and obstinate?

"How do you mean?"

By way of explanation, the cop pointed to the blue of the harbour below, the water shimmering in little heat waves and making Skorzeny narrow his dark eyes so that he could see fully. "The Red Cross seaplane."

"What of it?" Skorzeny asked puzzled. The white-painted hospital plane had been anchored in the outer harbour away from the German section ever since he had arrived on the island.

"It's gone."

"Yes, I can see that."

"And you know why?"

Skorzeny could have punched the happy Italian cop in the jaw. He was enjoying this interchange with the big German, especially as it was making out that Skorzeny was a lumbering, dull-witted fool, who couldn't see the obvious even when it was put right under his big *tedeschi* nose.

"I shall tell you," the cop said, obviously tiring of the game now and wanting to get out of the hot afternoon sun. "This morning, just after dawn, I was one of an escort party taking someone down to that Red Cross plane. By the time the port was waking up and wondering why a plane was

taking off at that ungodly hour, it was already on its way
– back to the Motherland. And you know who was on that
Red Cross plane, German?" he ended, winking at the others.
"Well, I'll tell you. It was the man that your doctor friend
told you was dead. Seemingly he must have done a Jesus
act and risen from the dead."

"You mean *Mussolini*?" Skorzeny roared. But he didn't
finish the sentence. He whirled round, as if jerked thus
by an invisible wire and surveyed the whole bay. It glis-
tened as if painted with some kind of enamel. But it was
empty, totally empty of any kind of plane. The damned
macaronis had done it again. They had snatched Mussolini
away at the very last monent. All hopes of a dawn rescue
of *il Duce* vanished in an instant. They had failed once
more . . .

Seven hundred kilometres off La Maddalena, the two officers savoured the evening breeze, strolling slowly around
Rome's Ciampino airfield, Student smoking his cheap after-
dinner cigar, while Geier, the Vulture, favoured a specially
made cigarette, smoked through a long ivory cigarette
holder. At a respectful distance behind them, the duty
officer, Kuno von Dodenburg, followed, a little bored by the
whole business, for his mind was on the fighting in Sicily.
Any day now it would be over – the Italians down there
were deserting in their thousands to the Anglo-Americans.
It could be only a matters of days, perhaps hours, before
the enemy started landing on the Italian mainland and the
only thing which could throw them back into the Straits of
Messina would be an immediate armoured thrust into their
beachhead – and that thrust would have to be conducted
by SS Assault Regiment Wotan if it were to succeed. For
that reason, these games they were all playing with the

missing Mussolini didn't interest him one jot. Now only *action* counted.

He turned his attention to them again and caught Student saying – 'barking' would be a better description, for he never seemed to say anything in a normal tone – "My guess now is that, unless the spaghetti-eaters are going to hand him straightaway to the Anglo-Americans as a token of good faith, they'll move Mussolini closer to Rome, the centre of Italian power."

"*Genau, Herr General,*" von Dodenburg heard the Vulture say and he could tell by his CO's tone that he was bored, too, as he was by most things. "Which will make me a rear echelon stallion with a nice comfy office in Berlin, where I can devote myself to my other – er – *interests,*" as he was wont to confide in his few cronies. "But where exactly? Rome itself is a rumour-factory, as you well know, General. In the capital, you wouldn't keep Mussolini's hiding place secret for very long."

Student paused in his stride and nodded gravely. "I agree. Therefore it has to be close – the hiding place, I mean – yet cut off and relatively hard to approach. In confidence, Colonel Geier, I have approached the commander of one of our Junkers 52 squadrons, based at Lake Bracciano, about fifty kilometres north of Rome. I'm going to ask him to keep a discreet lookout for that missing Red Cross plane Skorzeny reported, or any other plane entering Rome air space without proper authorisation, not only from the macaronis, but also from our own people."

"Excellent idea," Geier agreed without enthusiasm.

Von Dodenburg knew why. This was the Italians' own country. Surely they'd know ways to hoodwink the German newcomers, even if this unknown Junkers squadron leader *were* on the lookout for the missing Italian leader. The young armoured commander stopped listening again and prayed the two speakers would turn in for the night soon. Otherwise they'd go round in circles like this for ever.

His wish was granted. Suddenly, a cyclist came hissing into view, his bike lit only by a shaded blue lamp. *"Herr General,"* he cried, *"Wo sind Sie?"*

"Over here. Where's the fire, man?"

Hastily the panting orderly braked to a stop, sprang to attention, chest heaving with the effort and gasped, "Top priority, *Herr General.* Message to you – *your eyes only* – from *Geschwaderführer* Lenz at Bracc—"

But Student was no longer listening. With surprising speed and agility for a middle-aged man running to fat, he had wrenched the bike from the surprised soldier's hands and was peddling for all he was worth towards the nearest hangar.

Hastily Geier stubbed out his cigarette and said out of the side of his mouth, "Well, my dear von Dodenburg, there we have it. Let's hope this one isn't going to be another damned wild-goose chase."

But in the background, von Dodenburg knew instinctively that this time it was not going to be; for at the edge of the field, he could hear the first throaty rumbles of drivers trying to start their 400 HP Tiger engines in the sudden cool of the August night. No, this time it was for real.

Chapter Seven

Thwack!

Schulze, as hot and sweaty as he was in the stalled convoy on the dead-straight, blinding-white road, winced at the sound of the bullet striking soft human flesh close by. Instinctively he flashed a look to the maize fields to left and right. Nothing. But then the tall stalks of maize could hide an army.

"What the hell was that?" Matz asked, voice crackling metallically over the intercom from the Tiger's driving compartment down below the great ten-ton turret.

"How should I know?" Schulze snarled. "Am I—" The words died on his lips. Their troop leader, *Fahnenjunker* Dietz, who had been standing arrogantly in the turret of his Tiger, the very epitome of a future masterful SS officer, was slowly beginning to crumble, his hands sliding from their hold on the metal. He opened his mouth to say something. Nothing came save a sudden spurt of bright red blood. An instant later he hit the steel deck, dead before he did so.

For what seemed a long moment, the tankers of SS Assault Regiment Wotan simply stood there, motionless in their turrets like waxworks frozen for all time. Then von Dodenburg, at the head of the long column heading south, shrilled on his whistle three times. It was the signal they

64

were all used to, the 'old hares' who had served in Russia. *"Partisanen!"* they cried urgently.

Swiftly the panzergrenadiers baled out of their half-tracks to left and right, surging into the golden dusty fields of maize immediately and without a single order being given. They all knew the drill. They had carried it out often enough.

At the same time every fourth tank swerved out of the column and with a great flurry of earth and pebbles from their massive tracks, followed suit, their long overhanging guns moving from left to right like the snouts of predatory monsters seeking out their prey.

The Vulture looked back. There was no fear on his ugly face, just concern. *He* was not going to die at the hands of some local peasant turned partisan. Von Dodenburg waved and he nodded in return. Let the young fool risk his turnip, if he was that eager for glory. Von Dodenburg didn't hesitate. He grabbed his Schmeisser, clicked off the 'safety' and dropped neatly over the side to join the attack force.

Led by the tanks in a great armoured V, their tracks churning up the maize into a golden pulp which floated in their wake like a yellow cloud, the sweating young panzergrenadiers searched for the man who had fired the single shot, while on the turrets of the tanks, the gunners swept their machine-guns from side to side ready to open fire at the slightest sign of trouble. It was standard operating procedure, well exercised in Russia with its vast partisan hordes who constantly attacked the German invaders 'supply columns.' 'Use metal, not men', was the motto, which meant, blast the partisans to hell with overwhelming firepower rather than than risk men's precious lives by doing too little. And at the end of the dangerous exercise there had to be a visible punishment for treacherous attackers – a score of bodies hanging from the nearest telegraph posts as a grim warning to the others.

But so far, von Dodenburg told himself, trying to ignore the hot beads of sweat running down his crimson face, there's only been one of the back-stabbing swine—

He broke off suddenly. It was almost as if his words had whistled up more trouble. To the far right, a light machine-gun had opened up abruptly. Tracer sped across the tops of the maize in a white flurry of flying steel. Someone screamed shrilly. A panzergrenadier dropped his weapon. He clapped his hand to his right eye socket which was suddenly empty. Five metres away from him another grenadier grabbed the air frantically, as if attempting to climb the rungs of an invisible ladder. To no avail! His face turned upwards as if pleading with some god on high to save him, he fell backwards, right into the flailing tracks of a panzergrenadier half-track. What reappeared in the suddenly scarlet tracks was a severed hand, waving back and forth with the motion of the carrier, as if bidding them goodbye.

Von Dodenburg bit his bottom lip, sickened. He opened his mouth to shout a command. Schulze, the old hare, beat him to it. "Hit the tube!" he yelled over the intercom. Matz needed no urging. He surged through the twenty-odd gears of the seventy-ton tank. It picked up speed immediately.

Von Dodenburg hesitated. In Russia he would have broken off the action immediately. There the partisans, happy that they had caused a couple of casualties among the hated 'Fritzes', would have started withdrawing before the German murder squads caught up with them. The Italians, new to the underhand tactics of the partisans and their attackers, might think differently and continue the action. Thus there might be a chance of taking prisoners, who could be 'squeezed' for information before they faced the inevitable necktie parties. What should he do? Should he continue?

Next moment the decision was made for him. As Schulze's turret gunner started to spray the maize in front of him with incendiary bullets, already beginning to set it alight to smoke out anyone hidden in it, a half-track, some twenty metres to the rear of the Tiger, bucked sharply like a wild horse being put to the saddle for the first time. Thick white smoke started to rush from its ruptured engine and to ascend to the perfect blue summer sky. One minute after that green and white flares sailed into the air from the Vulture's command tank. It was the signal for recall.

Von Dodenburg waited no longer. Time was running out. The Vulture wouldn't have recalled them for anything unimportant. He glanced at the monstrous hulk of Schulze's Tiger crashing through the maize like a crazy harvester. He told himself that the big rogue wouldn't get caught with his knickers down. He would head for the stunted olive groves to his left front, driving whatever opposition he found in front of him. There the partisans would have to disperse if they wanted to continue living – the cover was too sparse. Then Schulze would veer right, make a dogleg and join the column further up the road. Von Dodenburg knew the big NCO. He could take care of himself.

The harshly handsome young officer, his rakishly tilted SS cap shoved to the back of his yellow cropped head, cried into the throat mike, "All right, you Christmas tree soldiers . . . Move it . . . *NOW!*"

With the tanks firing smoke from the dischargers on both sides of their turrets and effectively covering the great lumbering shapes, they and the panzergrenadiers started to back off out of the field and onto the dead-straight road. To their front Schulze's Tiger and the handful of grenadiers who had clambered aboard disappeared into the smoke screen – and the unknown.

"What's that damned fool Schulze up to?" the Vulture snapped, looking down at a sweating von Dodenburg. "Is he trying to cure his throatache or something?" He nodded at the coveted Knight's Cross of the Iron Cross hanging from von Dodenburg's neck.

Von Dodenburg thought it better to remain silent. Not that Geier objected to his men winning medals for bravery. They all added to the elite reputation of Wotan and anything which did that meant he'd achieve his general's stars more quickly. Inside the Vulture's command tank the radio continued to squawk incessantly. Evidently there was something important going on, von Dodenburg told himself.

"Let's forget the fool," the Vulture went on. "If he ends up looking at the potatoes from beneath the earth, well, it's what he deserves. Von Dodenburg," his harsh rasping voice rose.

"Sir?"

"I've just had an urgent signal from General Student. We're to turn about immediately – forget the Lake – and return to Rome P.D.Q." He gave the younger man a wintry smile. "Pretty damned quick to you."

"What's the hurry, sir?" von Dodenburg asked, confused, head cocked to one side listening intently for any firing in the fields to his rear. But there was none.

"Don't know, frankly. It was an open line and naturally they weren't able to say very much except for what I've just told you. But you can guess, can't you?"

"*Mussolini*? They've found the Duce?" von Dodenburg replied.

"Yes, something like that, I suppose, and you can be

sure it's not too far away from here, von Dodenburg.
Otherwise they wouldn't ask for our help. With these
roads and mountains – and now those damned scallywags
of partisans – it'd take Wotan a good day to cover eighty
miles, and this is a very long country indeed."

Von Dodenburg nodded his understanding. He strained a
little more and told himself that he could hear some faint
shouting in the wood which was now a long way off, but
there again, in combat one imagined many things.

The Vulture said, after a moment's hesitation, "One thing,
Kuno." When he was in a good mood he often used the
casual 'thou' and the first name of his officers; otherwise
it was strictly the formal 'you' and the military title.

"Sir?"

"It's pretty clear – at least to me – that those two, Student
and Skorzeny, are strictly glory-hunters. Ever since the
failure of his airborne attack on Crete in '41, Student of the
paras – the Victor of Holland,' he uttered the words with a
contemptuous twist of his thin sensual lips, "has been out
of the limelight. As for Skorzeny – he is an unknown, who
somehow got the Führer's ear. Now," he went on as von
Dodenburg stared up at him puzzled, wondering where all
this was leading, "both of them will try to outdo the other
in order to gain the kudos of having rescued Hitler's friend,
Benito Mussolini. It will be elbows all the way," he jerked
his skinny elbows back and forth in the German gesture for
those who try to push themselves to the top. "So where does
that leave Wotan?"

Von Dodenburg didn't answer. He was concentrating on
the faint sounds in the woods; and this time he knew he
wasn't imagining them.

"I shall tell you," the Vulture answered his own question.
"Out in the cold, if we don't damn well do something about

it." His thin raddled face flushed a sudden red as if he were very angry. "But that is not going to be as long as I have a breath in my body. If anyone is going to come out of this nasty business smelling of roses, it's going to be Wotan. Is that understood, Kuno?" He glared down at the handsome young officer through the monocle he affected, though he didn't need it. "Regardless of losses and hardship, SS Assault Regiment Wotan will be seen by the great German public as the rescuers of Mussolini. *Klar?*"

"*Klar, Obersturmbannführer,*" von Dodenburg rasped woodenly, his face revealing nothing, his mind racing. It had started already. If Schulze didn't find his way back out of the possible trap by himself, he'd be written off. Indeed, as the Vulture started to rap out his orders for the column's return, von Dodenburg knew with a sense of helplessness that Schulze had been written off already.

Chapter Eight

Schulze cursed fluently as he peered down the gloomy trail through the wood of stunted olive trees and straggly parched bushes. Now he couldn't hear the others. They had fled deeper into the trees before their German attackers and by now, Schulze guessed, in the manner of all partisans, they were heading for their villages to take up the cover of ordinary hard-working peasants.

From down below in the hot stifling Tiger, Matz said, "What's the problem? Flank the shit and let's get on with it. It's getting dark and I want to get back to Mummie."

Schulze growled. He was caught in a quandary. If he advanced down the narrow trail to take out the lone sniper, he risked losing more of the panzergrenadiers guarding the Tiger on its steel deck and on the ground to both sides. If he took off to either flank, he might run into mines or tank traps that could immoblise the metal monster. He knew the cunning tricks of the partisans of old; they were up to all sorts of devious dodges.

For a long moment there was a heavy brooding silence, broken only by the steady throb of the great Maibach engine like the beat of a metal heart, while he made his decision. When he did, it was one that cheered up Matz in the steel driving compartment no end. "I'm gonna back off," he announced, obviously disgusted with himself for having taken the easy way out.

"That's it, old house," Matz said heartily. "Let's take our hindlegs in our flippers and do a bunk." Before he was ordered to do so, he rammed home first gear and revved the mighty engine. Up the trail the Italian sniper heard the noise and from his leafy hiding place, aimed and fired in one and the same movement.

Viciously the slug howled off the thick metal of the turret next to Schulze. The latter jumped and cursed. "The Eye-tie fired at *me!*"

"Well, he wasn't inviting you to dance with him cheek to cheek," Matz commented unfeelingly, and pressing hard on the huge accelerator increased the great tank's speed in reverse.

In that same instant the unknown sniper fired again and struck lucky. The slug penetrated the driver's slit, shattered the glass prism of one of the amplifiers to Matz's right and drove an ugly sliver of thick glass into the little man's wizened cheek. The lucky shot caught Matz completely off guard. He yelped with pain and instinctively twisted the steering wheel to one side. It was an unfortunate move. There was a sudden empty whirring which was the bane of tankers' lives all over the fighting fronts. The tank lurched alarmingly. A moment later there was a metallic slithering noise like an anchor chain being released – and the Tiger stopped dead, its massive engine roaring impotently. It had thrown a track.

Some twenty kilometres away on the road to Rome, the convoy, too, had come to an abrupt stop. But it wasn't due to enemy action. Instead a Feisler Storch monoplane of the *Luftwaffe* had appeared out of nowhere, firing signal flares as it descended to use the road itself as a runaway; moments later, with the engine barely stopped, two familiar figures were running towards the Vulture's command tank, waving their arms like crazy men.

A few moments later they were turfing a barefoot Italian peasant family out of their tumbledown hut near the road, trying to ignore the black stare of the grandmother, whose toothless face was withered like a mummy's shrunken skull by sun and hard work. Outside, the rest of the peasants, grouped around their moth-eaten donkey, their only possession of any value, stared at them with reproach – poor scarecrows, riddled by disease and malnutrition, victims of man's inhumanity to man.

But the new arrivals had no eyes for the peasants, turfed so rudely out of their home which stank of poverty. They were too eager to impart their great news to the Vulture and von Dodenburg.

"We thought it wouldn't have been wise at this stage of the game for the locals to see that you had been recalled," Student said urgently. "Hence the meeting here."

"Yes, the peasants are all informers," Skorzeny chimed in. "Here no one can observe us."

The Vulture thought he might tell the excited couple of officers about their recent brush with the partisans, but then decided against it.

In the flickering yellow light of a petroleum lamp and that of their own torches, the four of them stared down at the map spread out on the rickety kitchen table and anchored by means of two bayonets,

"The Gran Sasso," Student announced and swept his hand over the map. "A hundred kilometres south of Rome and in the centre of the Italian Appennines."

Von Dodenburg wrinkled his eyes and tried to make out the heights and contours and the effect they would have on military operations.

Skorzeny, to get into the discussion, beat him to it. "The Monte Corno above the Gran Sasso is the highest peak in the Appennines. It is crowned with snow summer and winter."

Student frowned, but hastily took up the explanation himself before the Austrian could continue. "Here, some nine kilometres below the Monte Corno is the Campo Imperatore Hotel, a favourite with those who come to the Gran Sasso to ski. The sole access to the hotel is here – a funicular which runs five thousand sheer metres up from the village of Assergi, here."

"But what has this all got do with us?" the Vulture protested, angry that the other two appeared to be doing all the running.

Student beamed at him with his mouthful of yellow tombstone teeth. "What? I'll tell you. Because we have good reason to believe that Mussolini is being held in the Campo Imperatore." He held out a slip. "Here, look at this for instance. It's a translation of a message in Italian picked up by our people yesterday."

The Vulture took it and held it at an angle to the yellow light so that he could see it better while the taller von Dodenburg peered over his shoulder. '*Security precautions round Gran Sasso d'Italia have been completed,*' he read.

An excited Skorzeny could hardly wait for them to finish and he broke into their perusal with, "Our agents tell us that checkpoints have been set up everywhere down at the hotel. Angry locals say that the old staff of the place have been fired without notice. And here's a very curious thing. When my people started to look for maps and tourist literature of the place – you know, that highly-coloured junk stuff – there wasn't a single item to be found. *It had all disappeared, lock, stock, and barrel!*"

"*Jawohl, Herr General,*" the Vulture growled somewhat

grimly, addressing Student pointedly. "It does seem as this really *is* Mussolini's place of imprisonment."

"I am sure of it one hundred per cent," the latter replied, "especially if you visualise the difficulty of attacking the hotel."

Outside, the peasant scarecrows had knelt, holding the shabby donkey's head down as they did so that it appeared the whole family, including the animal, were kneeling at prayer. Von Dodenburg felt sorry for them, but in the fashion of his type and time, he told himself cynically: God has long been looking the other way. He had no time or sympathy for such pathetic creatures as they were.

"In essence," Student was saying, "there appears to be only one link between the village Assergi – here – and the Hotel Campo Imperatore – here – and it is this kind of lift, perhaps a ski lift. Anyone who controls it controls the approach to the hotel – and Mussolini. And we must assume, gentlemen, that if the Italians who are holding him are alerted that there is any kind of danger threatening their captive, they will deal with him immediately." Significantly he drew a forefinger across his throat. *"Like this."*

The others frowned and abruptly there was no sound save the quiet chant of the Italians praying and someone urinating in a hurried gush somewhere in the darkness. Finally Student broke it with a cynical, "Gentlemen, somehow I think we'd better start praying too."

Chapter Nine

Schulze tensed in the green darkness of the wooded glade. He looked around. At the stranded tank they were ready. They had greased all the connecting nuts and, before they had switched off the engine, run the track out behind the Tiger so that it now lay there like a broken metal limb. Around it were the two beefiest men of the cut-off section, sledgehammers muffled with cloth, at the ready, eager to start work once Schulze gave the signal. Around the tank group, the rest of the panzergrenadiers crouched in a semi-circle. They provided a rough-and-ready perimeter defence. Once the racket started, Schulze guessed he'd need them and their firepower; for it would be then that the Eyeties would attack, alerted to the fact by the noise that the metal monster was a harmless cripple.

"Jetzt'geht's los," Schulze whispered to Matz standing near to him. The little corporal would take over while he was gone. "And keep your glassy orbs skinned," he added the warning urgently.

"Like a can of peeled tomatoes," Matz replied. He lowered his voice even more and there was genuine warmth and concern in it when he spoke again, "And watch yer back, old house. Treacherous lot them foreigners."

Schulze was moved too but he didn't show it to his old running mate. Instead he whispered, "Don't lay it on so thick, Matzie – yer'll have me crying in my beer next. Give me five minutes. As soon as you hear my signal, get that track pinned up, tootsweet." And with that he was gone, moving with surprising speed for such a big man.

Matz breathed out hard and prayed that nothing would go wrong, for he realised that their position here deep in the Italian wood with the crippled Tiger was dangerously exposed. Then he dismissed the problem the best he could and turned to the others. "All right, you lot," he snarled, "get ready to get to work as soon as I give the signal, or it'll be the worse fer yer." Then the little corporal settled down to wait for Schulze.

Stolidly, making surprisingly little noise, Schulze moved forward through the sparse grass and gnarled branches, now both heavy with dew. Every few seconds he cocked his head to one side and listened intently, but there was no sound, save the occasional bark of some hound a long way off and the steady chatter of the cicadas. It seemed that he might well be the last man alive in the world. But old hare that he was, his senses sharpened by years of constant combat, he knew instinctively that wasn't the case. There was someone out there surely. He crept on through the wet grass, occasionally slapping at the mosquitoes which were now beginning to plague him.

Hastily he ran over his impromptu plan again. As soon as he spotted them, he would take up a defensive position and give Matz his signal to start work. In the night silence the sound of a sledgehammer striking a tank tie-pin would carry for kilometres. Once the partisans heard it and, realising that the Tiger was crippled and therefore relatively useless, began to move into the attack, he'd let them have it. With a bit of luck he'd be able to put them off their stroke long enough for the tankers to repair the track. "Then, old house," he whispered joyfully to himself, "it'll be off and home." He dismissed that happy thought almost immediately he had thought it. First he had to spot the wop partisans and lure them into this deadly trap.

Time passed with leaden feet. Carefully Schulze threaded his way through the undergrowth, Schmeisser at the ready, holding the machine-pistol in his huge paw like a child's toy.

Once he tripped on some kind of root and fell heavily, stifling his cry of rage just in time. He rose, grabbed his gun and pushed on.

Suddenly he stopped, sniffing the air like some hunting dog, abruptly becoming aware of the scent. He turned his head slowly, trying to pinpoint the aroma of cheap tobacco, the black kind the Italian peasants smoked. It was coming from his left, perhaps twenty metres or so away, from behind a thick glade of olive, glistening a shining grey in the dew.

Schulze hesitated, then he made his decision. He'd find out what the opposition was like before the balloon went up. It would be wiser that way. He started to move forward once more in the direction from which the pungent cheap tobacco smoke was coming, Schmeisser clutched at the ready. The moment of truth was almost upon him.

Now it was silent as death itself. He strained. He could hear nothing. Was there really someone out there? There *must* be, he told himself. He could still smell the tobacco. He came level with the glade. He pulled aside the nearest bough. He caught himself just in time as he was showered by the cold drops of dew. Nothing! He hesitated and then entered the glade, hardly daring to breathe as he did so. The smell was getting stronger and now, for the first time, he could hear the faint sound of voices like those of men being overly cautious that they were not going to be overheard.

In the far corner, clearly outlined by the eerie cold light of the sickle moon which had just risen, he could see a little group of civilians, crouched on their haunches, supported by their ancient hunting rifles and *lupuri*, listening intently to what a tall man was saying to them in a hoarse whisper. He screwed up his eyes and tried to get a better picture of the man.

He certainly *was* taller than his squat peasant listeners and his refined shaven face didn't look very Italian; indeed there was more of a northern German or even Englishman about it. And unlike the peasants, he was standing upright instead of squatting. Later Schulze would find out why – the man couldn't bend to any degree due to some sort of leg injury which made him limp. But at that moment Schulze wasn't very interested in the man's physical disabilities. He was more concerned with what he was instructing the peasants to do next – and he had an uneasy inkling it wasn't to be anything good for the men of Wotan.

Still, he had made his plan and now the time had come for him to carry it out, come what may. He placed his Schmeisser down momentarily, pulled a pistol and a stick grenade out of his jackboot – these would be supplementary firepower just in case anything went wrong – then taking up his machine-pistol once more and giving the magazine one final slap to ensure it was in place, he cried with all his strength, *"Now!"*

Suddenly, things started to happen in rapid succession. There was the hollow boom of metal striking metal – that was the sledgehammer being wielded against the kingpin. A hoarse cry of surprise from the tall man with the limp. Yells of anger from the partisans and then the cry *"Avanti*

... *avanti* ... !" Next moment, as the partisans rushed forward in the direction of the sound, Schulze opened fire from the hip, swinging from side to side like a gunslinger in a Hollywood Western, spraying lead in an angry fury at the Italians. The battle had commenced.

Matz didn't waste any further time. As the shout was followed almost instantly by a wild outburst of firing inside the forest, he yelled, "All right, Alfonse – *hit it!*"

The trooper needed no urging. He knew that they had only minutes at their disposal now the partisans were alerted. He swung his hammer and slammed at the side of tie-pin in the track raised and held by half a dozen of the other troopers. Their bodies trembled under the impact. But the tie-pin remained obstinately in place. The trooper grunted, spat on his burning palms once more and swung the sledgehammer again.

Meanwhile Matz, crouched in position, eyed the wood, as if half-expecting a bunch of wildly yelling partisans to burst out of it, firing from the hip, at any moment.

Metal struck metal once more. The track vibrated angrily. One of the assistants almost dropped the chain track with the pain of the impact. In the last instant, with hands that seemed to be on fire, he held on to it. "For Chrissake," Matz yelled, besides himself with impatience, "dig it out of the orifice, trooper. We ain't got all the time in the world."

Up front the firing was intensifying and Matz could hear the high hysterical bursts of Schmeisser fire which indicated that Schulze was fully involved with the enemy. He said a quick prayer that the NCO would not be carried away by the crazy excitement of battle and forget when to break off the action.

The man swung his hammer again. This time the solid chunk of metal striking metal was replaced by a sudden clatter. Without looking round, Matz knew what had happened. He had succeeded in dislodging the tie-pin. "Up the cups!" he yelled exuberantly, using the old toast from the Russian front. "The night's gonna be cool. Keep up the good work."

Schulze agreed. Under the direction of the tall Italian with a limp, the Italians were attempting to slip by him to each flank. Grimly, he sprayed the bushes on either side, carried away by the crazy logic of combat, yelling, "Come on your dogs – do you want to live for ever?"

Now the crew at the crippled tank were pulling out the pin and hammering it straight, working all out while the rest poised with the raised track, ready to thread it over the bogies and lock it together once more.

Matz, trying to forget Schulze carrying out his one-man war as planned, hauled himself back into the steel driving compartment of the Tiger. He pressed the starting button. A low whine. Then nothing. He yelled out in sudden rage and slammed his fist against the steel plate painfully. "Now the motor won't work. God in heaven!"

He tried again, while outside the crew took the strain, thrust the spike through the heavy chain-track and with a grunt of unison lifted it to waist height. The back-breaking business of hauling it round the first bogey ready for rejoining of the broken piece was about to commence. But in order to get that track, which must have weighed a couple of tons, round, they needed the assistance of the motor. Desperately, the sweat standing out on his forehead, Matz kept his thumb on the starter button. Nothing came save a dull keening, which kept an even level, but which refused to spark and start the seventy-ton steel monster. "Come . . . come," Matz pleaded fervently. "Come – please – come for old Uncle Matz."

But the reluctant, stubborn engine remained unresponsive. Next moment there was a noise like a steel bar being run down a length of rails. Matz knew what that was. Naturally the salvo wasn't aimed – the men outside would have reacted if it had been – but it did mean the partisans were getting closer. Feverishly he pressed the damned starter button again.

Chapter Ten

Rome was in a state of chaos.

For the first time Mussolini's 'new Romans', who days before had cheered and mobbed the hot streets when they had first heard of the fact that the Duce had been deposed by his own fascist bosses, realised what that disposal really meant. Overnight Student's tough paras in their desert fatigues, each soldier strung with weapons and long bands of machine-gun ammunition, had appeared everywhere in the capital. Every street corner in central Rome seemed to be manned by them. Smoking sourly, grouped more often than not around machine-guns and their new top secret automatic rifles, they watched the sullen-faced civilians cautiously, as if they expected trouble at any moment. Low-flying German spotter planes circled the capital incessantly, while in the ministries around the Piazza del Viminale, the civil servants, sweating like they had never sweated before, continued to burn secret documents just in case – and everyone knew what that 'case' would be if the worst came to the worst.

Rumours spread far and wide. Rome was agog with them. Even those who still remained loyal to the vanished dictator, explained patiently, "*It is not the end of fascism. Indeed it has nothing to do with politics. The Grand Council deposed the Duce. It was because of a certain disease.*" Here the dark eyes of the teller would roll significantly – knowingly. "*You know how the Duce used to bed all those young women of his. Now he is hideously deformed – so much so that he has to be hidden from the Italian people, especially at this time of crisis, si?"*

Others were not so kind. The Duce had fled to Switzerland where he had great wealth stacked away as everyone knew . . . He had disappeared to the remote jungles of South America where "He'll stay till the storm blows over . . ." "Hitler has hidden him in a remote castle in the Alps. He is guarded night and day . . ."

Some maintained that the Duce would be brought to trial once the Allies signed an armistice with Italy. The reason? The Anglo-Americans wanted to show the Germans what would happen to *their* Führer, once he fell into their hands. Perhaps this would give the anti-Hitler factions the courage to get rid of Hitler while there was time.

One or two of the wiser rumour-mongers would add sagely, "But it won't end there. The Duce is no fool. He has a dossier on them all – Hitler, Roosevelt, de Gaulle, *Churchill*. Once he's brought to trial he'll spill the beans on all of them. Mark my words, it's going to be the biggest scandal of the twentieth century, that is," they would conclude, pulling down the corners of their right eyes in the Italian fashion to indicate caution. *"If the English, the perfidious English and that Mr Churchill of theirs, allow the Duce to live that long . . ."*

The weary Wotan column rolled into Rome that morning, a city groaning in another heatwave, with the skinny-ribbed dogs gasping in the dirty, overflowing gutters and the early morning shoppers sticking to the shade as they bought their bread and papers. Von Dodenburg, in the second tank behind the Vulture's, could see all the signs of an impending crisis. The Vulture had warned them to be on the lookout and ready for instant action. But von Dodenburg didn't need to be told that — the looks of hate, the hissed curses and once a thrown cobblestone were enough. The city was ripe for revolution. At the moment, it was only the presence of Student's parachute division which kept the lid on it. Once that division moved elsewhere, probably south to fight the Anglo-American invaders, Rome would blow up.

The Vulture's squawk came over the intercom. "Keep tight formation everywhere," he intoned metallically. ". . . Grenadiers ready for instant action. Use board MGs as last resort . . ."

Von Dodenburg caught him just before he was about to sign off, with, "Anything from Schulze, sir?"

"No," the other officer replied without feeling. It was typical of the CO. Schulze had served his purpose. He had been expendable, so why waste any further thought on the missing NCO and his young crew? Von Dodenburg bit his bottom lip angrily and choked back a furious retort. "Thank you, sir," he said and took his fingers from the throat mike. What did the Vulture care about men who died for him so that he could achieve the general's stars he craved? *Nothing.* His men were simply cannon fodder, necessary stepping stones on his way to the top. God, how he wished he could command Wotan. He'd fight to the last drop of blood to save the lives of these fervent young volunteers, National Socialist to a man, the best Germany still possessed after three years of war: the Fatherland's only hope for success in the future.

A brick slammed into the side of the Tiger as it rolled round a corner. A figure doubled away into the darkness of an old courtyard, even before von Dodenburg could draw his pistol. He shook his head like an infinitely weary man and, forgetting the Vulture, concentrated on wondering where those two rogues Matz and Schulze were at this very moment. He knew instinctively it wouldn't be long now before the Regiment would be needing tough old hares like them.

"Roll on death," Schulze said grandly, taking another swig of the weak Italian wine, "and let's have a go at the angels."

"Not yet, not yet, *please*," Matz said, thrusting his hand deeper up the fat, giggling, drunken whore's skirt. "If I'm going to die, let me die happy." The whore jumped, startled, and nearly upset the bottle of spumanti from which she was drinking.

"Hit the spot . . . hit the spot – just like that!" Matz chortled and clicked his fingers in triumph.

Schulze looked at his flushed happy running mate sourly. "So what?" he commented.

Matz ignored him. Instead he continued to paw the fat whore whose great breasts were already hanging out of her low-cut dress. "Marry me . . . oh, do marry me, my beloved, I can't live without you."

In response the whore, who didn't understand a word of what the German was saying, belched mightily.

Schulze sighed and told himself that although a stubble-hopper might well get a nasty self-inflicted wound in a knocking shop like this, with its screaming whores and dusty hams and salamis hanging from its beamed, smoke-grimed ceiling, it would be worth it. He took another of the gold coins they had found in the pocket of the dead partisan and tossed it to the cross-eyed, evil-looking landlord of the inn, whose gaze was everywhere, watching and calculating, as if he had a built-in cash register in his head. "More boozo," Schulze cried in what he thought was Italian. "*Molto birra* and firewater."

"*Si si, subito,*" the little landlord hurried away as fast as his little legs could bear him to carry out the NCO's orders, happy with the gold coin. Everyone in Italy was rejecting paper notes in favour of gold that could be used in the bad times obviously to come.

At first, after the partisan had died, after the firing had disappeared in the distance and the party had realised they were safe, the landlord had looked suspiciously at the gold coin that Schulze had offered him in return for women and drink. He had turned it over in his dirty paw several times, bit it more than once and then, giving the obverse a stiff rub, had stared at the design revealed there. Finally he had announced in Italian almost triumphantly, "Horse of St George – *Inglizi.*"

It was only later that they had discovered what he meant by the words. It referred to the design of the horseman, rider and dragon, which meant the coin was a British sovereign. But there was no mistaking his joy as sovereign after sovereign began to change hands as half-drunken troopers staggered upstairs with the paid-for blowsy whores.

As Matz stumbled up the stairs with his 'beloved', fondling her ample sagging buttocks lovingly, a puzzled Schulze again asked himself what the scruffy little dead macaroni had been doing with a purse full of Tommy sovereigns? There seemed no reason to it. "A little pip-squeak like that," he said half aloud in his bewilderment, "wouldn't even have a pot to piss in. So where did he get the green moss?"

But in the end he gave up. There seemed no answer to that overwhelming question. Instead he signalled the landlord to come over. Mindful of more gold to be earned, the landlord came at the run and hastily Schulze outlined a female figure in the air and shook his head at the drunken overblown whores. "Nix whores," he explained. "*Ragazza* . . . *bella figura* . . . Titties but no gut. *Capito*?"

The landlord *capitoed*. "You, my daughter?" he asked . . . Nix ficki-ficki. Virgin?"

Schulze clapped his big paw to his forehead as if aghast and simpered, "A virgin . . . *a virgin*! I didn't think that there was such a creature left in this world, even in a nunnery. Bring her on, old friend . . . BRING HER ON – AT THE DOUBLE . . . Tonight, come what may, I shall die a happy man . . ."

The landlord, his mind's eye full of those golden 'Horsemen of St George', which would see him through the two years of conflict to come in Italy, hurried away as if the devil himself were after him. A moment or two later, Schulze could hear him upstairs hurriedly awaking the 'virgin' with cries of "*Subito . . . molto d'oro . . . AVANTI!*"

He sighed contentedly and said to no one in particular, "What a funny old life it is. One minute up to her hooters in crap – the next it's all sweetness and light and strawberries for breakfast . . . It's something the old stubble-hopper is entitled to at least before he's getting his stupid turnip blown off." With that piece of infinite wisdom, Schulze leaned back in his rickety chair and took a long satisfying slug at his *grappa*.

A mile or two away in the heart of the pine forst, the tall man decided what he should do next. He had dismissed the amateur partisans, the minority communists, the rest paid by him to engage in a little banditry, though the latter hadn't realised just how dangerous it was. The tall man told himself cynically they'd learn fast enough – *in blood* – in the years to come. He had hoped simply to take one of the Germans prisoner. That would have simplified matters and in no way endangered his cover. Obviously this SS unit – Wotan, or whatever it was called – was involved, together with Student's parachute divisions, in the German reaction to Mussolini's disappearance. But how? What were the Jerries up to? He had thought even a simple German soldier would have given him the information needed. His amateur partisans, even the blood thirsty communists, already talking of 'blood running in the gutters' and a new 'Soviet Italy', would not have been able to tackle the handful of Germans in a defensive position such as the inn.

He frowned at the sickle moon and the silver-tinged clouds chased across the night sky by the wind. What was he going to do next? He didn't want to expose himself too much. Sooner or later his cover would run out if he did – and he had been taking hair-raising risks for months now. The Germans, who would soon be in charge in Italy, would waste no time with the likes of him. It would be the firing squad – or worse – at double quick time.

He sighed and made his decision. The Great Man was, he knew, relying upon him, and the Great Man's reputation was more important, in the long run, than his own life. *He* was Britain and the British Empire. For his part, he was a minor cog in the machinery. No one would miss him. His mind made up, he set off on the long slog back to Rome, knowing full well that he might be walking into a death trap.

Chapter Eleven

It was Saturday 11 September 1943.

Outside yet another German glider was coming in to land. Slowly the pilot had circled on the thermals until he judged he had been in the right position. Now he was coming in at treetop level, fighting to keep his wings straight – one false move and the big glider would be shattered into a thousand pieces.

In the briefing room at Pratica di Mare, the others forgot their planning, and watched the unknown pilot's progress with bated breath. Every glider was needed for what was to come. They couldn't afford to lose a single one. They groaned. The DFS 230 had hit the deck. In a flurry of dust, which obscured their vision for a few vital moments, it disappeared from sight. But when the dust cloud had vanished, there it was, hushing in at zero metres. Hastily the pilot avoided a gnarled tree which seemed to have appeared from nowhere. Next moment he had struck the ground. There was a rending, tearing sound of metal and canvas under tremendous pressure. The great bundles of barbed wire placed around the glider's wheels to slow it down began to burst like rotten twine.

Moments later, in a great wild swerve, throwing up a huge dust wave, the glider shuddered to a stop and the pilot dropped out on legs which felt like jelly.

Student nodded his approval. "Another one," he announced. "Just two more to go and we have our full complement of gliders and pilots."

All about him the others at the crucial briefing fell silent. There was tension in the very air of the tight room, guarded by heavily armed paras walking their beat on the outside, on the lookout for the first sign of trouble. For in the capital, only a few kilometres away, trouble was increasing. Smoke was ascending to the hard blue sky in slow mushrooms and again there was the sporadic angry chatter of gunfire. It was the Blackshirt Militia, who were still loyal to their Duce, fighting both the Italian Army and, where they could get away with it safely, odd patrols of the Parachute Corps.

Student took out the wet stump of his cheap working man's cigar, the ten pfennig ones that he affected, and cleared his throat to attract their attention. The officers, from the SS, Paras and the Luftwaffe's Glider Corps, turned to look at him.

Student commenced hesitantly. "Naturally I must point out first that we are basing our plan of attack on relatively defective information, because the latest information we possess about the Gran Sasso is already some days old."

He let the words sink in for a moment. "Whether Mussolini is there is uncertain. The Italians have a knack of spiriting him away each time, just before we are going to strike, eh Skorzeny?"

The SS man nodded and von Dodenburg wondered whether Student had referred to Skorzeny because he wanted to make it clear that it might well be his fault that the Duce had escaped yet again.

"Now then, at twelve hundred hours precisely tomorrow – Sunday. In essence it's going to be a three-part attack. From the air," he nodded to Skorzeny. "You and your tanks on the ground, Colonel Geier, in a flank guard role. With my paras etcetera taking and using the funicular lift to join the airborne attacks at the hotel. Everything will depend upon split-second timing and the exact step-by-step attack itself. We want no one firing upon friendly troops. We don't want the Italians to bogus down so that reserves can be dropped to them from the air." Student paused and frowned momentarily, as if he had become aware for the very first time of the complexity of the plan to be carried out scores of kilometres from the nearest German military installation. If they ran into difficulties, they would have to rely exclusively on their own resources to get out of the mess.

It was a thought that occurred to von Dodenburg for the first time, too. Suddenly he knew he was up to his neck in one of the war's riskiest operations. In essence it all depended upon the twelve HE 126s towing a dozen frail gliders. Each of these light, fabric-and-steel tubing structures would carry, in addition to the pilot, ten armed men made up of Student's paras and Skorzeny's SS commandos. Exactly one hundred and eight men to rescue the man who had once been the second most powerful dictator in Europe.

But he could see that the magnitude of their task didn't worry the commanders particularly. Their gaze was set firmly on the glory of the operation. If men were to die to make it successful, that would be no concern of theirs; they wouldn't be the ones who were doing the dying.

Student spoke again; he was his usual paternal self. "Keep your nerve. This operation will be conducted as a peacetime manoeuvre. Our surprise will be so great, believe you me, that the spaghetti-eaters will probably not loose off a single shot. All you have to do is to concentrate where you land and keep to your landing place. The rest will fall into place of its own accord." He smiled winningly at them.

The Vulture wasn't impressed. Neither was Student. He had crash-landed a glider back in 1920. He knew all the risks, but it was Colonel Geier who put them into words. He took his eyes off a blond glider pilot who could not have been a day over twenty. "I should think if the *carabinieri* at the base of the funicular are quick off the mark," he announced, "it would prevent any attempt to help those in the hotel itself in case they run into trouble." He frowned and adjusted his monocle once more.

Skorzeny cursed to himself. He didn't like the arrogant SS Colonel, nor the thick-headed para General for that mater. But soon, if he had his way, he would be the hero of the day and the two of them would be relegated to the obscurity from whence they had come.

"An aerial reconnaissance?" the Vulture suggested. "Then we might be able to see what the Eyeties have on the ground."

Student shook his head firmly. "Out of the question. The Führer has banned such recces. Though we have taken a risk and run two overflights, hasty ones. On the first the angle had been too bad. On the second we were too high for clear detail." He shrugged. "Anyway those damned Anglo-American terror fliers have knocked out our development lab at Frascati. All we can do is prepare smudgy prints. No good to pilots really."

Again they lapsed into silence. Von Dodenburg craned his head to study the photographs they did have. They weren't encouraging. The smudged photos revealed what looked like a lunar landscape where the gliders were supposed to land. Everywhere there were rocks and the angle was tremendous, the whole placed scarred by white seams of torrents that ran in a zig-zagging, purposeless direction. He could just make out a strip of what looked like tarmac, which might have been used for parking hotel visitors' cars. At all events, it seemed the only likely landing site. He frowned. This time, he told himself the tick-tock was really in the pisspot on the Gran Sasso.

So the briefing continued without any great enthusiasm on the part of those present. The imponderables, they now realised, whatever Student said to the contrary, were very great.

"My people," Skorzeny was saying, "will seize the hotel and the captive – there will be no firing unless we're alerted by the firing of a red Verey flare. Meanwhile," he nodded to Student, "your paras, sir, will come up from the village of Assergi and seize the funicular station and hold it against all comers—"

Suddenly von Dodenburg was no longer listening. His attention was elsewhere, as was the Vulture's as he cocked his ugly head to one side and tried to make out the sound coming from the perimeter, which was manned by Wotan. Finally the CO made his decision. "Check," he mouthed the word noiselessly.

Hastily von Dodenburg nodded, seized his cap and slid out of the briefing room, unnoticed by the rest. Now in the inky darkness, he could hear the sporadic snap and crack of a firefight to the east and see the tracer zipping through the night with lethal intensity. There was the sound of vehicles, too, many vehicles.

Von Dodenburg hesitated no longer. Something untoward was going on at the perimeter. There was no time to be wasted. He swung himself onto his borrowed motorcycle and hit the pedal hard. It roared into immediate noisy life. Next moment he was whizzing away towards the sound of the firing.

*   *   *

"We're in trouble now," Matz breathed as he stood in the Tiger's turret next to Schulze, who was manning the machine-gun – just in case.

"You can say that again," Schulze agreed, as he watched the long Italian column come to a stop. Someone had turned the spotlight on the Italians and the two old running mates could see that these men didn't look like the average scared Italian conscript soldier. These were tall, bronzed, muscular men and all wore the German and Italian parachute badges.

It was the badges that sparked off the recognition in Matz's mind. "The wops are from the Folgore Parachute Division," he explained. "We trained 'em in Germany and they fought alongside the Afrika Korps in the desert. Tough babies they're supposed to be."

"They're Eyeties, aren't they?" Schulze growled, as if that were explanation enough.

Just then von Dodenburg appeared out of the night, braking hard to avoid one of the stalled Italian vehicles and coming to a stop with a dramatic flourish. Schulze knew why. Voice full of admiration, he whispered out of the side of his mouth, "Get that, Matzi. Outnumbered a million to one and the Old Man knows just how to put the spaghetti-eaters in their place. They're impressed by that kind of thing."

Von Dodenburg propped up his bike, taking his time, observing the massed Italian parachutists out of the corner of his eyes and asking, "Trouble, Schulze?"

"Not yet, sir," the man whispered back.

Von Dodenburg nodded. To the rear, tracer was still zig-zagging back and forth across the night sky and fires were beginning to burn now. It was obvious that if there was no trouble here – just yet – there was plenty to the rear of these Italian paras who had appeared out of nowhere. Von Dodenburg took the bull by the horns and decided it was time that he did something. He took a deep breath and, taking his time, appearing to be almost casual, he started to walk over to the largest group of paras, grouped around a small half-tracked vehicle.

An officer stepped forward and saluted. Eyes flashing angrily in the eerie red light of the flares which now ascended into the sky on all sides, he said in a thick Italian accent, "I no speak very well . . . We have come to help Papa Student—"

Hastily von Dodenburg remembered that Student was a father figure to his paras, whatever their nationality. Behind his back they all called him 'Papa'. He nodded his understanding.

"We . . . not traitors like rest," the Italian spat angrily at the ground. "We fight with German comrades—"

"The Folgore have mutinied," a clear incisive voice, speaking perfect German, cut into the discussion.

Von Dodenburg looked to his right. A tall middle-aged man – to von Dodenburg he seemed middle-aged – had pushed his way through the crowd of Italians in their camouflaged uniforms and stood there. He was dressed in the full uniform of Mussolini's Fascist Militia, complete with ceremonial dagger and tasselled black cap. "Who are you?"

The militia officer ignored the question. Instead he snapped, like a man used to giving orders, and having them obeyed, "We had the devil's own job of getting through to your perimeter, *Obersturmführer*. As soon as they recognised the Folgore, especially in the working-class estates on the route, firing broke out immediately." He indicated the firefight taking place to the rear. "Communists and rabble like that, of course. We should have been harder to them before the War." He shrugged eloquently, as if to indicate it was too late now. "Anyway, here we are now. General Student must tell us where he needs us. He can rely on the Folgore."

The officer who spoke some German agreed fiercely, his dark eyes flashing dangerously.

Somewhere close by yet another flare exploded with a soft plop and a crack, throwing the militia officer's face into full view for the first time. Von Dodenburg frowned. He had seen that face before, when the man hadn't been wearing a uniform, but where? The man showed no sign of recognising him. Dammit, he cursed to himself, who was he?

But before he could attempt to prove the matter further, the militia officer touched his hand to his cap and said, "I shall speak to our General now. Perhaps you will ensure that he has safe passage through your lines to General Student, where he will presumably be given further orders." And before von Dodenburg could stop the man, he had pushed his way through the burly paras and was limping off into the darkness.

Mr Yates and Colonel Pitman

Yates rubbed his eyes wearily. He ached all over. But it had been worth it. What the little maid had lacked in sophistication in bed, she had made up for with her energy. It had been a long time since he had had sex with a woman who couldn't get enough.

Now, his bones creaking audibly, he tumbled out of the great rumpled bed. Downstairs the grandfather clock in the gloomy hall chimed eight. It was time to get ready. Old men, he knew, didn't sleep late – their bladders wouldn't allow them to do so. Besides they had nothing to snuggle up to. Christ, he told himself, as he looked at the bed and wondered where he should start first; it was tough to be old.

He spotted a pair of rumpled black briefs underneath the coverlet. Hastily he grabbed them and dropped them into his suitcase. They would give him something to think about on his lonely nights, and journalists of his kind spent many lonely nights in scruffy hotel bedrooms all over the world. They had to have something to take their minds off the sheer lonely boredom of it all.

Yates dismissed such thoughts as he finished tidying up the bed and opened the stiff windows, which didn't appear to have been opened for years, to drive out her smell of cheap scent. He had to get on with this business with Colonel Pitman. After all Jenkins, the editor, had snapped, "Okay your hunch is good. But the skipper won't sub you for more than three days on the Continent. He says – as he always does, the miser – that we're not made of money." Every hour was precious.

Hastily as he shaved and then dressed, he ran over what little he knew. Pitman had obviously been in the Med in the

War, though he wasn't sure he had been in Italy. Still, he thought it very likely, especially now as he remembered what those upturned blue-and-white wings, that Pitman and the rest had been wearing on the photo with the foreign woman, meant. They meant that Pitman – one could hardly believe it today, the condition he was in – had made three combat jumps behind enemy lines. So, it seemed that as a young officer, he had been in either the SAS or perhaps more likely the SOE, the wartime intelligence service which Churchill had ordered to be created with the rallying cry: 'Let them set Europe alight!' *That they had certainly done.*

Further, the old boy, with his cunning, rheumy eyes, had admitted he had been in Venice in the early fifties. Now why should a lowly military attaché be invited to meet the Great Man? Yates frowned at his image in the flyblown old mirror. The bags under his eyes were almost septic. "That's what comes from making whoopee," *he intoned the old Eddie Cantor song of the thirties under his breath. The answer, he thought, was obvious. It was something that Pitman had undertaken during the War – probably in Italy – which had created a bond between him and the PM. But what and how did it fit into the puzzle which Jenkins had landed him with?*

For a moment he thought with envy of the Sunday Times *Insight team. God, he thought to himself, what I could do with something like that backing me up. But then, he concluded, the rag he worked for wasn't the* Sunday Times, *with a boss like Murdoch, who could afford to keep correspondents in every European capital and who could trot out ex-PMs, poncey Oxbridge profs and professional pundits at the drop of a hat.*

There was a soft knock at the door and the girl's voice said, "Frühstück, mein Herr."

"Damn it," he cursed. *"Now she's speaking German."*
Yesterday it was French. God knows what she would be
speaking on the morrow. "Enter," he cried.

She did so, carrying a big tray heavy with the cold cuts
they served for breakfast, including a great chop of smoked
cold pork, plus the dark, floury rolls of the area. "Der Herr
bittet Sie um acht Uhr funfzehn," *she said formally. But*
as she went out, she bowed and flung up the back of her
short silk maid's dress to reveal the trim, bruised buttocks
beneath. He grinned. She knew about the knickers then. That
night promised to be a hot one again . . .

"Morning, Yates," the Colonel's voice was sharper and
clearer than before and Yates suspected he had had a drink
of his 'medicine', as he called his Scotch, to get him started
for the day. He was tucked in an antiquated wheelchair, with
an iron driving tiller and basketwork sides that looked like
something out of a 'Folk Museum'. "Ready to go. You can
push," Pitman commanded. *"Better that way. Just you and*
me. After all," he added, seemingly apropos of nothing,
"just one witness is no *witness, what."*

A little confused Yates agreed and then with a little help
from the servant in the green baize apron, they negotiated
the contraption outside into the cool fresh morning air.

Hesitant and wondering how he should start, feeling
something of a fool – what would the other guys think if
they could see him pushing a bathchair now; they'd probably
laugh him out of El Vino's – he shoved Colonel Pitman up
the steep incline. They passed farmhouses and cottages, most
with water pumps and great piles of steaming manure out-
side the kitchen door. "The bigger the shitheap, the richer
the owner is supposed to be by the other locals," Pitman
explained. Here and there, villagers in blue overalls stopped
when they saw the Colonel, took off their peaked caps and

murmured "Morje, Colonel," *a greeting he acknowledged like a royal with a wave of his hand. "They respect me, the English milord," he explained. "Tell all sorts of wierd and wonderful tales about me."*

"Bit out in the boondocks, Colonel," Yates ventured.

"Boondocks? . . . Yes, I suppose it is, but it suits me. Away from it all. The minority here amounts to sixty thousand souls. They have absolutely no political power so neither Brussels nor Bonn is interested in them. Even the teachers and their priests come from elsewhere and most of them don't even speak the lingo. It makes confession hell for the natives."

Yates thought he saw an opening. Panting, for the going was steep, he asked, "So why did you pick the place? A good place to get away, sir?"

Colonel Pitman didn't seem to hear. Instead he raised his stick from beneath the plaid rug covering his frail legs and pointed to the base of the hill next to the little stone bridge under which the river marking the border ran. "That's where von Dodenburg – you've heard of him? – assembled his battle group ready for his dash during the Battle of the Bulge. The Yank historians write it was further downstream. Rubbish! Bits and pieces of his stuff marked '1944' can still be found there."

Yates got it. The old man was playing games with him. First it was the German commando leader Skorzeny and then this SS guy von Dodenburg, who was sentenced to death after the War, but who had also been involved somehow in the affair. He looked down at his charge, but the thin, pinched, grey face revealed nothing. So he tried again, a little desperately. "All the same, sir, it must be pretty lonely for you in this neck of the woods. No clubs and stuff," he ended a bit lamely.

"I am not one bit interested, Mr Yates, in what you call 'stuff'. Stuff sickens me, makes me wish I'd never been born an Englishman, well, half an Englishman."

The bitter outburst was so sudden and so out of character that Yates started. *"I don't quite understand, Colonel,"* he stuttered – and he genuinely didn't.

"I'll explain," Pitman said, controlling his wrath with difficulty, his thin, dying face suddenly flushed hectically like that of someone suffering from a high fever. *"I was born into a country of which I was proud – much more than the other one which is in my blood too."*

The remark puzzled Yates but he said nothing. At last the old boy seemed to be opening up. With luck he'd give him the lead he'd come all this way to get. Perhaps then Jenkins would leave him in peace.

"I know you'll think this – your generation always does – the sounding off of the old-buffer generation. But we lived in an ordered society with institutions that we could respect – and did so. Now, what have we got?" He waved his stick, as if he was having difficulty in finding the right words because he was too angry to do so. "An Empire that vanished, handed to the wogs on a silver platter so that they could loot it, as they have been these last fifty years. A monarchy that certainly won't last another fifty years; cut off from its citizens, playing games as if they were some bloody, thick-skinned German princelings. And a Church of England made up of bloody middle-aged frustrated spinsters and nervous nellies of four-eyed bloody pansies!" He paused for breath after so much effort and Yates could hear the air wheezing in and out of his smoke-raddled lungs as if through ancient, cracked leather bellows.

"But Colonel—" he began.

The angry old man beat him to it. He pointed to the sign at

the end of the village, posted over the blue-and-white village limits mark. It depicted a wolf-like creature with its teeth bared ferociously. Underneath the depiction there was the legend in bright red, reading in German – ACHTUNG – WILDTOLLWUT – GEFAHR!

"Attention – Danger of rabid wild animals," the Colonel translated, his voice calmer now. Indeed the sign seemed to please him in a mysterious sort of a way. "Rabies, crossing Belgium and Northern France at a rate of four kilometres a year. It's already been found in foxes in the Pas de Calais, around the port. Won't be long now before it crosses the Channel into the UK proper." He chuckled. It wasn't a pleasant sound and Yates felt a cold finger of fear trace its way slowly down the small of his back.

"So," the Colonel continued as Yates started to push the creaking ancient carriage forward once more. "If we don't wipe out what's left of our proud heritage ourselves, then the rabies might do it for us. But at all events, those few great men who survive in our folk memory will have to be protected from harm at the hands of lesser people till it all goes finally to pieces."

Yates was angry suddenly at the old man's oblique approach, his warnings of doom and gloom. He was typical of all those old people, your 'Disgusted of Cheltenham' types, who still couldn't realise that their *day had long passed. There were no more 'legends'. All of them had feet of clay. Even before he realised he was saying the words, he blurted out, "Is that why you're trying to protect Churchill?"*

Pitman didn't answer immediately. Instead he stared up at his carer, anger replaced by mild cynicism in his fading eyes.

Yates waited and then opened his mouth as if to repeated

his accusation, but the Colonel held up his clawlike hand for silence and said quite simply, "Yes."

"Why?"

"Because he's the only great Englishman to come out of the last half a century – and without feet of clay!" Fiercely he emphasised the words. "Why should I help you and that cheap gutter rag of yours to compromise him, I ask you?" He lowered his voice and there was an undertone almost of pleading in it when he spoke again. "Is there really nothing sacred still? After all, Yates, he did save our nation from a terrible fate back then. God knows what England would have been like if he hadn't saved us from defeat."

Yates was not impressed by the old man's pleading. He sensed he was coming in for the 'kill'. He had almost broken the crabby old bastard down. What did history and the 'Great Old Man' mean to him? Nothing! *All he was interested in was by-lines, banner headlines and bonuses. He knew that if he could unravel this ancient puzzle and produce the scoop that Jenkins and his socialist pals wanted, he'd be quids in. He might even get himself a cushy job in one of those TV documentary channels – the pressure off, months to complete the project and a job for life. "So you do know about this Churchill papers business, sir?" he snapped relentlessly. It was not a statement of fact, but more of a naked accusation.*

"Of course, I do," Colonel Pitman replied testily, as if he had recovered some of his old strength. "I'm not some old fart suffering from Alzheimer's, you know, and I still do have a few sources of info. You've come here to pump me. You thought you'd find a dotty old gent who had buried himself in a God-forsaken part of Belgium, which most Belgies don't even know belong to their country, who would roll over and allow his stomach to be scratched because he's got a visitor

– yes, a real live visitor!" *he added with old cynicism, "who was going to make him feel important again because he wanted information about the link between Mr Churchill, that crook Skorzeny and his puffed-up claims, and naturally poor old Musso. Didn't you?"*

Suddenly Yates realised he was losing control of the situation, just when he had thought he had gotten it well in hand. Hastily he protested, "Admittedly, Colonel, I thought you could probably supply me with some information on those lines. Our contacts and informants in London and Italy—" the rest of his words were abruptly drowned by the sharp crack of a high-powered hunting rifle. Once . . . twice . . . three times . . . He flashed a look at the Colonel, puzzled.

Pitman took the sudden shooting in his stride like the old soldier he was. "Eleven o'clock," he announced. "Just to the rear of the bridge where the meadow starts. Hochstand *– hunting blind to you . . . Got it? Fat, rich German hunter from Dusseldorf . . . So fat he can't get up the* Hochstand *ladder without difficulty."*

"Yes, I see it, sir."

There was a sudden crash. A large animal flew onto the loose gravel of the country road, struggled furiously, rose to its legs and staggered a few paces onwards towards the border with Belgium, as if salvation could be found there.

The old man squinted against the light. "Either our fat German has hit some poor old buck by mistake or the animal's rabid."

"Rabid, sir. It's foaming at the mouth," Yates stopped short as the big animal dropped to the ground once more and writhed in its death throes. From the bushes next to the wooded 'blind', a fat hunter, all in green, waddled, knife in one hand, hunting rifle complete with telescopic sight, in the

other. As he panted over to where the buck lay with heaving ribs and bright red blood dribbling from its gaping mouth, he had a stump of a nearly smoked cigar rolling from one side of his thick lips to the other.

"He's supposed to slit the animal's throat, now," Pitman informed Yates, who stared at the macabre little scene aghast. "It's the German hunter's duty."

Not this one. Perhaps he was worried about getting his expensive hunter's greens spoiled by the dying animal's blood. Instead he spat out his cigar, gave the animal a tentative kick with his hunting boot and then, shouldering his telescopic rifle, he turned back to German territory like a weary soldier returning from the wars. A moment later they heard the sound of his Mercedes starting up. He had had enough.

Pitman laughed drily. "Well, it's happened enough on this frontier in the past," he said thoughtfully. "Probably it will do again . . . Frontiers are simply dangerous places to be. I think we'll go back now don't you?" He smiled coldly.

Yates didn't protest. He had seen enough. Wordlessly he turned the carriage and, leaning forward, started pushing it up the hill back to the chateau. And this time he didn't protest against the effort. He was glad to get away from the place, for suddenly he realised that frontiers were dangerous, even for 'veteran newshounds' like himself. Anything could happen there – and no one would be any the wiser . . .

Part Three

THE RESCUE

Chapter Twelve

Dawn!

Above the snow-tipped peaks of the mountains the sky was already a hard wintry blue. Below, the snowcaps themselves were coloured a warm ochre. Further down still on the Gran Sasso itself the hotel was still in the shadows; the sun hadn't penetrated that far yet, and there was something sinister and almost threatening about the place. Von Dodenburg, lowering his glasses and yawning, told himself it was all imagination; it was simply because he couldn't see what was going on in the hotel where they were holding Mussolini.

Schulze came bustling up, his face wreathed in smiles, his breath smelling of strong spirits. In one hand he balanced a steaming canteen; in the other he had a thick hunk of salami crudely smeared over the surface of a big slab of grey bread. For some strange reason he was wearing a ladies' blouse, bursting at the seams, underneath his tropical uniform. He handed the canteen to von Dodenburg carefully. "Hot as hell, sir. Carefully does it. But there's nothing better than a steaming hot cup of nigger sweat," he winked knowingly, "laced with a certain forbidden substance, to set a front swine up for the day." The coffee was followed by the 'sandwich'. "Mule sausage, sir, and sawdust slabs. The best I could do for vittels, sir, I'm afraid."

110

"You look after me like an old mother hen, you big rogue," von Dodenburg said with a smile. "But thanks." He took a tentative sip at the hot coffee and wondered idly if the slug of *grappa* in it could possibly take the enamel off his teeth. All around them the tank crew prepared for the coming action – cleaning the long barrels of their 88s, refuelling, lugging great 100lb rounds into the shell lockers, tightening tracks: the hundred and one things that tankers had to do before battle. "Why the natty ladies' blouse, Schulze?" he asked.

Schulze hung his head in mock modesty. "An Italian lady in the village—"

"Some lady!" Matz sneered from where he sat, cleaning the dirt from his toenails with the point of his bayonet. "Had her drawers down in zero, comma, nothing seconds, as soon as she saw what you was prepared to offer her."

"*Offer her!*" Schulze chuckled. "Actually I'm thinking *seriously* of offering her my hand in marriage when this little lot is over."

Matz made a contemptuous sucking noise with his lips as von Dodenburg repeated doggedly, "The blouse?"

"Oh, well, sir, seeing it's Sunday I thought I'd tart myself up a—"

"Ah, there you are, Kuno," the Vulture's rasping Prussian accents cut in.

"Sir?" Von Dodenburg clicked to attention as did Schulze – *reluctantly.*

"Last minute instructions," the Vulture got down to business straightaway, taking his eyes off a bunch of the *Folgare* who, naked to the waist, were carrying out their morning ablutions, their bronzed upper bodies gleaming in the rising sun. "Anticipated arrival of air assault force zero eight hundred hours. The pilots of the tows will release their gliders over our recognition panels here. Once the gliders are down, we are to move in with the Italians and support Major Otto Mors—"

Von Dodenburg nodded to indicate he knew the tough parachute battalion commander who would be seizing the funicular and then leading his men up across the valley to take Mussolini out of Skorzeny's hands. Mors would then ensure that Mussolini was taken down to the plain from where he would be flown to the Reich in triumph in order to meet the Führer.

"Naturally," the Vulture added cynically, "Student wants the kudos of delivering the Duce personally to Berlin."

"Sir," von Dodenburg snapped woodenly, though he told himself that the up-and-coming newcomer, Skorzeny, might have other ideas on that.

"One last thing. There will be no firing unless absolutely imperative. That is the Führer's own order. At this stage of the business here in Italy he doesn't want to have things made worse by German troops firing on those of our country's erstwhile allies, though I for one cannot fathom what good the Italian Army has been to us since they joined us back in forty."

Von Dodenburg said nothing and the Vulture, sourly eyeing a one-legged Matz, who was still happy turfing out the dirt from beneath his nails, said, "Well, I'll be getting back to my tank." He pulled down the side of his eye significantly and used the old German expression for watch your step: "*Holzauge sei wach.* Somehow I don't think this day is going to end exactly as the – er – Victor of Holland has planned it."

With that he was gone and von Dodenburg, leaving his two rogues to take charge, strolled over to the Italian para officers, a few of whom could speak broken German, to ask,

"I say, what happened to your interpreter?" He saw the blank looks on their handsome dark faces, added, "You know the one – the officer in the uniform of the Fascist Militia."

The puzzled Italian officers shook their heads. "No militia with us," one of them explained. "We fighting outfit – front swine – not rear echelon stallions," he smiled as he managed to pronounce the difficult German words.

"But—" von Dodenburg began. He never finished, for everywhere in the lines of the Italo-German assault force, the cry went up, "*Here they come . . . here come the planes!*"

Von Dodenburg swung round with the rest, already raising and focusing his binoculars as he did so.

Silently, like a great twin metal V, the formation which was to attack the Gran Sasso came into view, flying steadily and purposefully towards their objective. Effortlessly they slid into the gleaming calibrated glass circles of von Dodenburg's binoculars. He started to count them – twelve twin-engined Heinkels, towing a dozen DFS gliders, laden with men, skidding and slithering from side to side, rising and falling startlingly as the first thermals from the mountains below caught them. But that didn't worry von Dodenburg and the rest of the observers. They knew that the gliders were piloted by the cream of the *Luftwaffe*, men who had won European championships back in the thirties when they had been mere boys back in the Hitler Youth. If anyone was going to bring it off, landing their heavily laden planes on the tricky mountain slopes of the Gran Sasso successfully, it would be they.

Slowly von Dodenburg lowered his glasses. Earlier that morning the news had been released that the Western Allies had landed in the boot of Italy. They were there in force. And von Dodenburg knew as soon as this business in the Gran Sasso was finished, no more time would be wasted by the Führer paying back old debts to pre-war friends. Wotan and the rest of the German armour would be rushed south to throw the Anglo-Americans back into the sea from whence they had come before it was too late; and *he* would be glad to be gone, too. What he desired now was a good clear-cut fight against the real enemy instead of all this office-seeking and attempts to curry the Führer's favour. Somehow he guessed there was more to it as well. In that very same instant he had recalled where he had met the mystery man with the limp, whom he had encountered the day before wearing the uniform of an officer of the Fascist Militia.

He had been the tall, distinguished civilian with a limp – he had just remembered, too, he had been attached to the Italian Legation in Berlin – to whom his cousin had introduced him at the Hotel Adlon. He recalled him well, wondering what the two of them had in common, apart perhaps from the pleasures of the bed together. Now for some reason, the distinguished Italian, who didn't really look like one, had turned up here in the middle of the bold rescue attempt dressed as a junior officer, before disappearing into thin air. It was rum, very rum. But before von Dodenburg had time to consider the mystery any further, the noise of engines starting in the Vulture's command group cleared his mind of the matter. The op was on. Now other things had priority . . .

Petulantly, like a thwarted child, Mussolini swept the solitaire cards from the breakfast table with an angry gesture of his hairy hand. Fat and unshaven, his black eyes dominating his sallow moonshaped face, he rounded on his new friend, the local farmer who reared sheep. "You and your damned prophecies!" he bellowed, scattering saliva everywhere as he did so. "You're trying to make a fool of me!"

Nisi, the gnarled old farmer, his new friend, regarded the one-time leader of Italy sadly, as they sat together in Room 201, the low-ceilinged single-room 'apartment' in the Hotel Campo Imperatore, that was now Mussolini's cell.

The two unlikely friends had met four days before and had gotten on well together. After all, Nisi was a peasant as Mussolini had once been in his youth. Reluctantly the commander of the guard had allowed the sheep-farmer to visit his former 'Leader' to pass the time of day. It was during one of these visits that Mussolini had discovered that Nisi had the backwood peasant talent of 'playing the cards'.

That morning Mussolini had begged Nisi to read his future in the cards – indeed he had refused his frugal breakfast until Nisi had given in. But the former Duce had not been pleased by what Nisi had told him, for the forecast read, 'You are to be rescued under romantic circumstances, *il Duce.*' Indeed the prophesy had so enraged Mussolini, still unshaven and unwashed, that he had swept the cards from the breakfast table in fury.

For Mussolini, the ex-master of Italy, was at the end of his tether. A couple of days before a group of children under the guidance of a nun had appeared out of nowhere and before the guards could shush them away, they had spotted Mussolini and saluted him with the fascist greeting until the nun had chided them gently with, "We don't do that any more, boys." That night he had tried to slash his wrists in an amateurish sort of a way with a blunt razor blade.

But unknown to Mussolini, as he glowered in sullen silence at the dirty wall opposite, this hot September day was going to bring about the reversal of his forture in a very romantic way. For high above the Gran Sasso at that very moment, a lone German Feisler Storch hovered over the cold stark-white spur of the Monte Corno like some strange metallic hawk. Hidden by the spur from the hotel below, the pilot from Student's elite parachute force watched and waited. But he knew he could not do so for much longer – his gas was running out. Down below at the Hotel Campo Imperatore all was quiet. People went about their routine duties quietly and without haste. "The Wops don't suspect a thing," the pilot told himself, in the fashion of lonely men who talk to themselves. "But where in three devils' name are the rest?"

His face underneath the leather flying helmet grew grim. He had lost contact with both the attack force and Student's HQ, somewhere down below, an hour earlier, and he didn't dare run a search over the radio in case the spaghetti-eaters picked up his transmission. He sighed like a man sorely tried and flashed a glance at his gasoline gauge. The needle was already flickering in and out of the red zone. He couldn't stay there much longer, if he wanted to reach his airstrip on the plain safely; and he didn't fancy attempting a crash-landing in these remote craggy mountains. He made up his mind: he'd make one last sweep and then, if he spotted nothing of the airborne assault force, he'd pick up his hindlegs beneath his armpits and buzz off back home.

He pulled back the stick and started to skim round the Monte Corno once more, using the updraught of the crosswinds there to carry him along with the least possible use of the engine; that way he'd save precious gas.

Suddenly his heart skipped a beat. He gasped. There they were – the rescue assault. But what had happened?

All he could see in the harsh blue sky were the stark black outlines of the towing planes, with two gliders bouncing up and down on the thermals behind them, their tow ropes stretched taut, as if they might well snap at any moment.

116

But it wasn't the snapping of the ropes that worried the lone spotter pilot. It was the fact that there were only two gliders here from the original assault force. That meant exactly eighteen paras were currently in position above the Hotel Campo Imperatore. He cursed and said aloud in sheer frustration, *"Eighteen of 'em simply can't do it!"*

Chapter Thirteen

"*Bloody Germans!*" Major Pitman cursed angrily, as he took his glasses off the long line of Germans and Italians rolling across the plain in a great wake of dust from their tank tracks, and focused them on the mountains. Down below the morning air was already beginning to ripple a light blue in the growing heat, making things difficult to pick out. But above the mountains, the air was still and cold. Everything there was outlined with stark clarity. It wasn't hard, therefore, to identify the handful of aircraft beginning to bunch over the Gran Sasso. It was the German airborne assault. He hadn't expected the enemy to attempt that kind of rescue operation – and with so few aircraft to boot – but he knew them well; after all, before he had been wounded with the Eighth Army, he had fought them in the desert for nearly a year. They'd have a go, however small their number.

He turned the glasses and focused on the huts and buildings around the funicular that led up the sheer side of the mountain towards the hotel in which they had imprisoned Mussolini. The area was full of heavily armed *carabinieri*. They were everywhere. But if they were expecting trouble, they didn't show it. Perhaps they hadn't spotted the dark, squat shapes of the planes hovering above them yet. At all events the paramilitary policemen in their smart uniforms were going about their duties in the usual slow Italian fashion. What did the Germans call it? *'Komm' ich heute, komm' ich morgen.* If I don't make it today, I'll do it tomorrow.'

His upper lip curled in contempt. How typical! He thought back to his prep school where he had arrived straight from Bolzano in '32. The other kids had ragged him mercilessly when they had discovered his second name was the Italian 'Gino', thanks to his *mama*. But he'd soon shown them he was English and the bullying had stopped after he had kneed Hawkins Minor in the balls. A few of them had said that had been 'un-English'. But he hadn't worried about that fact one bit. He had been satisfied that the bullying had stopped and they had started to take him for an English boy, pure and simple, especially as he had turned out to be a leading light in the house cricket team that summer. 'The demon bowler of St Ives' they had called him and it had not fazed him one iota when some of them had whispered that his 'googlies' were not 'altogether cricket'. For if there was one thing he had from his Italian heritage, it was: 'Forget fairness. It doesn't pay.' He had reassured himself often those days, when he had been a lonely foreigner in an English school, using the dreaded 'F' word to shock himself, and at the same time show them just how tough and devil-may-care he really was.

He forgot the past and the lazy Eyeties, and concentrated on the events soon to take place in the hotel, recalling as he did so those words – the final ones – the Great Old Man had addressed to him just before he had left for the Middle East again on his mission: "My fate is not important, Pitman. But *what* I represent is. For that reason you must take the gravest of risks." Now he was going to do just that.

Otto Skorzeny, in the second glider, was not a happy

119

man. Everything was going wrong, terribly wrong. What had happened to the rest of the airborne assault? The para leader had made a hand signal unknown to him and almost instantly most of the force had vanished into the clouds. Now, due to the thermals and other factors which he didn't understand, his glider was beginning to take over the lead and already up front their Heinkel was preparing to cast off the tow. In a moment they would be all alone: eleven men to rescue one of the most important men in Europe!

The towrope lashed the air like a great bull whip. Next moment the glider jerked downwards sickeningly. Suddenly there was a great hushed silence. Desperately Skorzeny and the paras, laden with weapons and equipment, grabbed for holds, their faces ashen under their rimless helmets. Peering through a tear in the fabric, Skorzeny saw to his horror that the slab of concrete, which they had hoped was an emergency landing strip and had cheered themselves up with the thought, was in reality *a main ski-run*! *"Himmelsakrament!"* he cursed and held on even tighter to his stanchion – they were heading straight for destruction!

Now they were skimming madly across the side of the mountain. Rocks, dirt and stunted bushes rushed by in a blur at eighty kilometres an hour. Up front, the pilot, his face lathered in sweat and contorted with fear, made a last moment decision. It was now or never. He jerked the stick back – the glider rose sharply. The men's stomachs seemed to float abruptly in mid-air as they were jolted back against their seats. Next moment the pilot threw open the braking flaps. It was a devil-or-dare moment. Either the frail glider would disintegrate under the tremendous pressure – already every piece of metal squeaked and protested against it – or the braking operation would work. The upturned nose and the huge brakes opened to full extent should slow her up enough, on this Valkyrie ride of death, to allow the glider to hit the deck, all 2,000 pounds of it, without falling apart.

The pilot waited, heart beating like a trip-hammer. Suddenly, shocking the pilot though he had been expecting it, the glider hit the rocky slope. Screeching madly it hurtled across it, scattering pebbles and dirt behind it in a great blinding wake. The strands of barbed wire wrapped around its wheels to shorten the landing distance snapped like twine. Holding on for all his life was worth, the sweating pilot steered it, using the last of his strength, half-standing in his seat with the effort, dodging obstacle after obstacle by a hair's breadth.

By now it was obvious he was in control. The huge glider was begining to slow down. A tree ripped at the port wing which came off like that of an insect. The glider started to yaw. The pilot caught it in time, the veins at his temples standing out. The tail splintered like matchwood. Stones ripped huge holes in the fragile canvas and then with one loud lurch, the glider, almost wrecked to pieces, came to a halt.

For what seemed an eternity, the paras slumped in their seats, unable to move, all energy drained from their tough, trained bodies, as if some unseen tap had been opened. Finally they began to stir. A man farted. Another began to retch and vomit into his helmet. At the shattered controls, the pilot leaned forward, relieved of his tremendous responsibility at last, and appeared to fall into a deep sleep.

Skorzeny shook himself carefully. Tenderly he felt his limbs, half-expecting them to be broken. They weren't. Blinking at the strong sunshine which was now pouring through the holes in the fabric, he started to clamber over the wreckage. He slammed his massive shoulder against the jammed door. It flew open. He stumbled to the outside, his

legs like jelly beneath him so that for an instant he thought
he might fall. He didn't. For there, less than twenty metres
from where they had landed, was the main portal of the
Hotel Campo Imperatore – and it was totally unguarded!
There wasn't even a porter in sight! It was time to attack
before the balloon went up.

Down in the collection of huts, kiosks and sheds which
surrounded the entrance to the funicular, the *carabinieri*
were getting ready and von Dodenburg, standing some way
off in his Tiger, waiting for the order to advance, could see
they knew their business. They'd already driven off the first
attack of Student's paras – there were dead German bodies
littering the area everywhere. Now they were preparing a
more solid defence and in some depth too. Snipers had
climbed to the top of the cable workshop and were lying
there, rifles at the ready, waiting to pick off the German
leaders when they came within range. Anti-tank guns had
been rolled up and dug in, prepared to meet the German
tanks if they attacked and naturally their infantry had ducked
into their prepared positions – bunkers, slit trenches and the
like – while a few brave engineers, risking the paras' sniping,
were stringing out barbed wire and setting out anti-personnel
mines which would slow down the next German attack. To
von Dodenburg's eye it all looked very determined and
professional.

As if to confirm his fears, the Vulture's voice came
crackling across the ether metallically, distorted by the
brass band music the Italian jammers were employing, to
announce, "Student's paras are about to go in again. Hold
off the tank attack until I give the signal. I don't want to
risk my tanks if I can get away with it, on this damn fool
business. Over and out."

Von Dodenburg, as he released his grip on the throat mike, frowned. He didn't like the order. The correct tactic at this moment was to go for the carabinieri like the men said – '*Ran wie Blucher*' – and give the Italians no chance to establish their positions in depth. For it would cost only more lives of Wotan's young panzergrenadiers to winkle them out in the end. He sighed and Schulze, being able to read his thoughts, said: "Rank hath its privileges, sir, you know." He winked knowingly.

"Oh shut up," von Dodenburg retorted, but there was no rancour in his voice, for he knew Schulze was right: the Vulture could do exactly what he liked with Wotan, as long as he made a success of it finally.

Time passed. Sitting in the shade cast now by the turret hatch, Matz, leafing through his French pornographic pictures, one of the 'consolations of a poor stubble-hopper's short life' (as he always put it), said lazily, "Like to keep me hand in, Schulze, yer know."

"Yes, I know," Schulze sneered, making an explicit gesture with his clenched fist. "But then," he shrugged carelessly, "that's all yer good for, ain't it?" He laughed coarsely. "Keep yer hand in, old house."

"I didn't—" Matz began to object, but von Dodenburg shushed him before he could finish.

"Hold your water, Matz. Listen." He cocked his head once more and heard again the faint crackle of pistol fire coming from up the mountain. "Skorzeny's in business."

The handful of paras sprinted from the wrecked gliders, heading for the hotel, machine-pistols clutched at the ready, belts crammed with stick grenades. Italian officers in the upper rooms, some of them still naked from their beds, began to cry piteously, "Don't shoot . . . For God's sake, don't shoot, comrades!"

A moment later, from his one-room apartment on the second floor, his bald, partially shaven head clearly visible, Mussolini joined in, yelling, "Don't shed blood, I order you . . . *Don't shed blood!*"

Pandemonium reigned, as the rest of the missing gliders came hurtling in at an alarming speed. They seemed to be everywhere, hissing through the air at zero feet, slamming into the rocky face of the plateau, slithering and skidding to a stop, shedding bits and pieces of the fuselage behind them, as the paras readied themselves for the mad rush out of the door or slits they had ripped in the canvas with their fighting knives. Above them the crazy roar of the tow-plane engines echoed and re-echoed around the amphitheatre of the mountains.

The Italians started to react. Wild firing broke out. Down in the cellars, the fierce watchdogs were turned loose and raced, teeth bared frighteningly, to meet the invaders. SS men and paras went down everywhere, some dropping for cover, others falling never to rise again. All was mayhem, murder and sudden savage extinction.

Skorzeny, followed by his tough bodyguard Sergeant Otto Schwerdt, clattered into the hall of the hotel in his hobnailed mountain boots. Through an open door they glimpsed an Italian signaller hunched over his set, furiously transmitting morse. The two German didn't hesitate. They rushed forward. The Italian turned in alarm. Too late! Schwerdt launched a tremendous kick at the transmitter, putting all his two hundred-odd pounds of bone and muscle behind the kick. In the same instant, Skorzeny kicked the radio operator's stool from beneath him and sent the man flying into the corner, a mess of tangled, bruised limbs.

They raced on and came to a blank wall some three metres high. It was too high even for Skorzeny's great height.

But the trained paras knew what to do. A NCO bent and took the strain immediately. Skorzeny didn't need a second invitation. He grunted and stepped on the NCO's back. Then it was the NCO's turn to grunt as his knees almost buckled beneath him under the Austrian giant's weight.

Panting, sweating, cursing, the Germans raced on, fanning out to find the Duce's room, for already they could hear the vicious snap and crackle of the firefight below as the SS troopers prepared to stop the Italians using the mountain lift to the hotel.

Skorzeny spotted some back stairs. Could they lead to the Duce's room? A slug slammed into the wall a metre away, showering him with stone splinters. He hesitated no longer. Two at a time, he sprinted up the stairs, possessed by the desire to be first to rescue the Duce. He realised the honours it would bring. From being an obscure captain of the SS he would be thrust into the world's headlines – a national, even international hero. He'd be the man who had saved Benito Mussolini.

Following his instinct, he flung a glance through the slightly open door of Room 201. The photo of the Duce's late son, Bruno Mussolini, framed in black on the sideboard, told him he was right. He flung the door open.

There he was – Mussolini, covered by two Italians in uniform. Skorzeny turned typically Viennese, using all that people's oily charm. He bowed and announced grandly, as the guards watched impotently. "Duce, the Führer sent me! *You are free!*"

The broken-down old man in stark black rose to the occasion. He rushed to the giant and, reaching up, started kissing him fervently, exclaiming between kisses, "I knew my friend Adolf Hitler would not leave me in the lurch." He kissed Skorzeny again and as he did so the latter calculated it had taken exactly four minutes to rescue Mussolini since the glider had landed. In those 240 seconds he had become famous – some would say later 'notorious' – throughout the whole of the world.

Chapter Fourteen

The British major lowered his binoculars for a moment. It was clear that the fighting on the Gran Sasso had ended – at least for the time being. He could see the tiny figures, stark black against the white face of the mountain slope, picking up the casualties and carrying them inside. They were moving in an unhurried fashion and didn't walk bent double, as they would have done if they had been under fire. Somehow he knew that the Germans had rescued Mussolini – and worse luck, he was still alive. Now the bad business would commence once more and although Mussolini personally was powerless, he still presented a danger. He bit his bottom lip and half-listened to the fight to take the funicular. After all, with the gliders all wrecked, that was going to be the only way that his rescuers would be able to bring Mussolini down and take him off to wherever his final destination was to be.

The thought made up Major Pitman's mind for him. Wouldn't this, he asked himself suddenly, be the best and perhaps last chance they would have of getting rid of the man? A dead Duce wouldn't be able to talk and that was what they feared he might well do. London knew Mussolini had no future as a politician; he was hopeless, compromised – a creature without power, to be used by the Germans as they wished. But he did *know* things – *too many things*! If he started blabbing now there would be no end to the scandals he could cause.

His mind made up, Pitman slung his binoculars over his shoulder and made his way through the shoulder-height maize to where he had hidden his motorbike and sidecar. It was going to be dangerous, he knew, but it had to be done. Moments later he was roaring away down the white country track, trailing a great wake of dust behind him.

Angrily von Dodenburg pushed his steel helmet to the back of his head, a red wrinkled line crossing his forehead where it had been. "Look at those poor devils." He indicated the bodies of the young panzergrenadiers sprawled out in the extravagant postures of those done violently to death. "Stiffs before they had a chance to begin living."

"Life, sir," Schulze began and ducked hastily as a salvo of machine-pistol fire ripped the side of the turret lethally. "The macaroni buggers!" he yelled and, lifting a grenade from his boot, lobbed it at the *carabinieri* who had fired almost carelessly. The man screamed high and hysterically as he was engulfed with smoke and dust. When it cleared he was lying on the ground like a limp, bloody sack, his head lolling like a child's abandoned football. One moment more and he disappeared altogether underneath the churning, suddenly crimson tracks of the great tank.

The dreadful sight took the heart out of the remaining defenders. The first one tossed away his weapon and raised his hands in surrender. Another followed. Two men rose behind their light machine-gun and kicked it to one side angrily, as if it were the fault of the weapon that they were having to do this. Then the real mass surrender commenced and the firing petered away, as the troopers from Wotan crowded forward to loot their reluctant prisoners.

* * *

Now Skorzeny had time to talk to Mussolini and think what he was going to do next. He knew he had perhaps only minutes to make a decision which could only bring the wrath of General Student down upon his head.

Mussolini had recovered somewhat too. When he spoke there was something of that pre-war bombast of his about his speech, the same bombast with which he had cajoled, bullied, enthused his people. Down below the paras prepared to ascend in the funicular and take over for Student, as Mussolini asked grandly, "And what are my Romans doing?"

Skorzeny looked down at him. He might be the Führer's friend, but he was the same little wop who had helped to take Imperial Austria's alpine territories from here.

Brutally, Skorzeny answered, "Your Romans, Duce? Why, your Romans are – er – *looting*."

Mussolini clicked his fingers in irritation. "I don't mean the looters," he snapped testily. "I mean the true Fascists."

Skorzeny wasn't prepared to let him off the hook, as his brain raced, trying to solve his problem. "We can't find any, Duce," he said and then he felt sorry for the former leader. His face had fallen and suddenly he looked an old man, sad and defeated.

Now the mundane matter of packing the Duce's few possessions took place, with Skorzeny supervising (for, Austrian that he was, he was well aware that people sometimes did desperate things at moments like this; after all, Vienna did have the highest suicide rate in the world). In the meantime, Gerlach, Student's own pilot, had appeared, having finally landed the reconnaissance Feisler Storch in the sheep pasture which Nisi tended.

He saluted with *"Heil Duce"* and then got down to

business. There had been trouble. In his two-seater plane he could just manage to take the Duce to the plain. Skorzeny would have to remain up at the hotel instead of accompanying the Italian leader from the plain to Vienna airport and then on to meet the Führer, as had been planned previously.

Skorzeny flushed with anger. Obviously Student was trying to cut him out altogether. The old paratroop leader 'Papa' Student would get the medals, the banner headlines, the great receptions. He'd get damn all after all his work to find the Duce. He clenched his fist impotently and then he growled to himself. "No, I won't."

"What?" Gerlach asked, looking at him horrified. "But *Sturmbannführer*," he protested. "The Storch is a two-seater. Besides you must weigh at least two hundred pounds. I've paced out that pig of a runway outside," he jerked his head in the direction of the former ski slope. "With that weight we simply couldn't make it."

Skorzeny fought him tooth and nail. If he didn't win now, he'd disappear back into the obscurity from whence he had come. It wasn't for nothing that he he had been a champion sabre fencer in his student days in Vienna; he knew how to hack and thrust with the best. "You're going by air," he cried. "How much flying time have you got? Suppose something happens to you on the way and you're killed, eh? If so, he's alone in the desert." He indicated the ashen-faced Italian leader who listened open-mouthed, gawping like a village idiot. "And if we never find him – and I fail in my sworn duty to the Führer – what do you think is left to me, eh?" He opened his mouth and pushed his long forefinger towards it like the muzzle of a pistol. "The officer's way – that's what's left. I would have to kill myself, Gerlach."

The pilot looked bewildered while outside the enemies of

an hour before, the *carabinieri*, and Student's paras laughed and joked and posed for the official cameraman. Gerlach stared up at the sheer cliff of the Monto Corno, tipped with snow. There could be no take-off in that direction. Instead he'd have to chance taking off with the dangerous north-east wind behind him. The engine would have to be going all out at full throttle, brakes on until the exact moment when he started to taxi forward. With luck the Storch would be airborne by the time the short runway petered out. If it wasn't, he'd go arse-over-tip over the edge of the ravine beyond. That would be that. Furious at the dilemma in which Skorzeny was placing him, he cried, "We don't stand a chance, Skorzeny!"

Skorzeny, eyes on the fame and glory to come, wasn't impressed. Hitler would never forgive him if he made a mess of the great rescue. Whatever befell the Duce, he would have to share his fate.

Gerlach gave in at last. Eyes blazing furiously, he rounded on the Austrian giant with, "Well, for God's sake come, if you must. But if something happens on take-off, it's my responsibility."

Skorzeny knew what that meant. Gerlach would kick him out of the Storch without further ado. All the same he knew he had won. He said easily, oozing Viennese charm once more, "Of course, my dear Gerlach. You're in charge. *Los.* Let's go . . ."

Suddenly, before they could leave, Mussolini came to life. He lifted up a battered leather suitcase-cum-briefcase, which Skorzeny had noted, without too much interest, that he kept by his side most of the time, and said, "I'll leave the rest of my baggage, gentlemen, to be picked up later. But this must go with me. Papers of state – vital papers, you understand."

Gerlach groaned. "But that's adding more weight to the plane, Duce. Are those papers so important?"

Mussolini lowered his eyes, as if he didn't want the other two to see the look in them, but Skorzeny, on the make as always, did. Those papers were damnably important – he realised that in an instant. But why? Why was the Duce, a pilot himself, who knew the dangers of overloading a plane, risking death for documents of state? There *had* to be more to it than that.

Outside Skorzeny could hear the screeching noise the steel cable made as it wound the funicular up the mountainside. More than likely Student would be in the first load of passengers. Naturally *he* would want to have his photograph taken with the Duce. As soon as he heard the Austrian's plan he would cancel it and he had the rank and authority to do so. Skorzeny knew it was time to be off. He grasped the case and was astonished at the weight of its contents. The Duce must think these papers very important, he told himself, to be lugging them about with him in his now frail condition. "Come on," he urged. "Let's be on our way. Who knows how the Italians will react in a couple of hours' time – or the English? They will surely have contacts to the Italian traitors by now."

Gerlach gave in. "All right, damn it. Be it on your head then. Off we go." He stormed out.

The Duce followed with Skorzeny carrying the precious bag like a porter. Outside the crowd called in Italian and German, *"Evviva . . . Heil Duce!"*

None of the three took any notice. Suddenly the full impact of what they were about to do struck them. In a matter of minutes they could well be dead, lying at the bottom of that deep ravine, every bone in their bodies broken.

Skorzeny clambered aboard first. His huge figure bent almost double, he crouched awkwardly in the passenger seat at first and then, as Mussolini followed in a black overcoat and black hat, he moved to behind the seat to allow the other man to sit down.

Behind the controls, squinting against the sun's rays, Gerlach sweated as he revved the little engine of the light monoplane. He released the brakes and opened the throttle. The Storch started to move forward slowly, jolting over the debris on the crude runway. The German paras snapped to attention and raised their right arms in the 'Roman salute'. Mussolini didn't notice – he was too preoccupied by what was to come.

"Hold tight to the struts," Gerlach warned sharply, but kept his eyes on the controls.

The speed of the little plane increased. Tensely, the men on the ground watched as it bolted and jumped ever closer to the edge of the ravine – and doom.

The sweat streaming down his taut face in rivulets, Gerlach lowered the flaps as far as they would go, raising the speed at the same time to 150 kilometres an hour. In the same instant, he yanked with all his strength, veins standing out at his temples, face puce, as he tried to bring the plane up. The process seemed to take an age. Suddenly the spectators gasped with shock. With an unholy jar the right wheel struck a rock. The left wing canted downwards. It looked as if all was lost. They were right on the edge of the precipice now. Next instant, to everyone's shocked surprise, the Storch bounced off the lip of rock at a crazy angle. The drive of death had commenced. The plane was plummeting to the valley below, obviously out of control. It was the end!

But it wasn't.

While Skorzeny collapsed momentarily and the Duce

started praying in Italian like he had not prayed to himself since he had been a village schoolboy, Gerlach kept his head. The plane fell and fell. In a few moments it would be all over. But Gerlach didn't give up. He pushed the stick forward, increasing the Storch's speed at the same time. His plan was bold and there would be no second chance of repeating it if he failed now. Anxiously, gaze glued to the speedometer, he waited for the slipstream to raise the wings' level. Then at maximum speed, he would be able to pull the plane from its horrifying dive of death. Then he had it. He jerked the stick back. The wings were level. At a mere fifty metres above the plain, he sailed on across tidy little farms and vineyards, translucent with golden grapes, heading for Rome.

Raising his head from his hands, the Duce sobbed in German, "Thank you . . . *thank you for my life . . .*"

Chapter Fifteen

"*Schon gut*," the Vulture rasped into the mike, eyeing the rabble all around him, still celebrating the rescue. "To all. Wotan to start road march south in one hour at thirteen hundred precisely. Order of Field Marshal Kesselring," the new German Army Commander in Italy, "personally. Move south and prepare to meet the enemy." He chuckled – an unpleasant sound when it came from him. "The Field Marshal promises us glory and gratifications – and for those of you who are so inclined, as much gash as you wish. Over and out." He smiled to himself. Perhaps, he thought, he'd ask for an Italian batman. Some dark-eyed, curly-haired peasant boy with soft hands who wouldn't ask too many questions and who would do as he was told. Afterwards, when he was tired of him, he would send him back to his native village. Or, if that didn't work, in the turbulent, confused fighting soon to come in the south, the boy might get killed. That would solve the possibility of subsequent scandal even more efficiently. He smiled at the thought. Life at war wasn't too bad after all. It had its earthy consolations . . .

"*Glory, gratifications and gash!*" Schulze repeated the CO's words after von Dodenburg. "That'll be the day. All the same, sir, I'll be glad to see the back of this place." Schulze frowned. "I'm just a simple soldier boy—"

135

Von Dodenburg grinned maliciously at the words. "Simple soldier boy – my foot!"

Schulze persisted. "Well, for a simple soldier boy, there's something I don't like about this kind of lark. All mixed up. You don't know who's gonna pat yer on the back and who's gonna stick a knife into it."

Matz nodded sagely. He had taken a water bottle off one of the dead Italians and was having quiet little secret sips at the powerful *grappa* it contained. Schulze looked at him hard and Matz said hastily, "Just water, old house. I've gone teetotal, yer know."

Schulze sniffed, but said nothing. Up above them on the turret, von Dodenburg thought he knew what they meant. He hadn't liked this business from the start. There was something – he sought for a word – nasty (it was the only one he could bring to mind then) – about it. He'd be glad to be off to the fighting front. It might be dangerous, but it had always seemed to him to be a cleaner place than the world of the civvies.

One by one the Tigers' engines burst into mighty life, filling the air with the stink of fumes, the very ground below them seeming to shiver and pulsate as if it had a life of its own. The first one creaked away with a rusty squeak of tracks, its pennant, the feared silver skull-and-crossbones of SS Assault Regiment Wotan waving. More followed. Then came the half-tracks, crammed with panzergrenadiers munching the chocolate they had stolen from the Italians like the half-grown schoolboys that they mostly were. Behind came the great ponderous trucks laden with the shells and ammunition for the battle to come. Finally they were gone altogether – and no one looked back . . .

Up on the high plateau, Major Pitman watched them, and

folded away his binoculars. As he did so he made an assessment of what he had learned in the past few days, since he had abandoned the Hotel Adlon, with a half-naked woman huddled in the corner and the Gestapo hammering impatiently at the bedroom door.

It was clear from the possessive way that Mussolini had handled the bulging suitcase-cum-briefcase – at that distance he had not been able to make out exactly which it was – that it was very precious to him. If anything did, it was *it*. Otherwise he would have fussed with much heavier luggage which might have contained such objects as precious stones and gold coins that persons of his ilk would need when they were on the run.

Already his bosses knew that the Fascist Foreign Minister Count Ciano, who was also Mussolini's playboy son-in-law, had spirited his personal diaries to Switzerland. There he had made it clear to those Swiss officials who worked hand in glove with the Nazis – and there were many of them (money meant everything in that country) – that he would use the diaries, with their intimate secrets about both Fascist and Nazi officialdom, including the Führer himself, to protect himself if he was threatened.

Obviously Mussolini would do the same if he found himself in a tight corner. So far so good.

But what about the Jerries? Was their action in rescuing the former dictator purely altruistic? Or did they know something of what he knew, too? So far from what little he could see of them and Mussolini through his glasses high above him on the Gran Sasso, they knew nothing. The big fellow had taken Mussolini's bag for a few moments and then handed it back dutifully as if it were of no importance to him. He sucked his teeth and told himself that there was nothing more than he could do now. It was obvious that as soon as Mussolini landed in the plain beyond he would be transferred to a large aircraft and whisked straight off to Germany, where he would remain firmly under Hitler's protection, and guard. The Germans could – and probably would – still have some use for the deposed dictator.

All the same as he moved through the shoulder-height maize back to where he had hidden the motorbike and sidecar, he felt a sense of angry frustration. He would have liked to have done more. "Now all I've done is a half-baked job," he murmured to himself, beating off the flies which were rising from the maize stalks to plague him. Somehow he felt he was letting the Great Old Man down.

He remembered that secret meeting, the one and only one that he had had with Churchill. 'C' of the Secret Intelligence Service had taken him to Chequers one late afternoon and introduced him to the PM, who was alone (though later he discovered to his surprise from 'C' that Field Marshal Smuts from South Africa, representing the Empire, and Lord Beaverbrook of the *Express*, whom he supposed represented public opinion, had been hiding behind the big arras all along, listening to the brief interchange. He guessed that Churchill had wanted to discuss the matter with these elderly statesmen after he had gone).

The conversation had been brief. Churchill had explained the situation between him and Mussolini, while 'C' had listened gravely, occasionally nodding his grey head as if he approved of the particular point, but otherwise saying nothing.

"This morning I talked to President Roosevelt, via the transatlantic cable," Churchill said. "He told me he wanted to win the Italian–American vote for his re-election. So," Churchill grinned, displaying his ugly false teeth, "he was washing his hands of the whole Mussolini affair. Mussolini and Italy were going to be my – er – pigeon, as he phrased it. Some damned pigeon! He advised that the quickest way to solve the problem was to have Musso killed when he fell into our hands."

Hard-boiled as he was, Pitman had been shocked by the casual way that these great men talked about murder.

"Naturally, my dear Pitman," Churchill had continued gently, "I shall not have recourse to that unless it is absolutely necessary." Suddenly there was iron in his voice and his old eyes flashed fire. "But if it does become necessary, I shall act without hesitation. However, the best thing would be to get those damn fool papers and letters back like that. I don't care a fig about my reputation," he clicked his fingers contemptuously. "Publish and be damned, as the Great Duke" – he meant his predecessor, the Duke of Wellington – "would say. Yet it is not *my* reputation which is at stake, but that of the King Emperor and his Empire."

Pitman had felt a shiver of both apprehension and pride run down his spine. He knew that those were not the empty, mealy-mouthed excuses of a professional politician. No, they were the words of a patriot.

"Bring me those papers, Pitman," Churchill had ended "and I – and the country – will be eternally indebted to you . . ."

A little morosely Pitman remembered Churchill's last words to him, as he waded through the maize field, sweating profusely and swatting at the damned flies, which seemingly had come from nowhere to torment him. Thus it was that he was too wrapped up in what he perceived his failure to notice the slight movement, some five yards to his front near to where his vehicle was hidden, just off the track. When he did, it was too late.

The two paras were obviously drunk and in a bad mood. "There's one of the macaroni arseholes," the bigger of the two snarled, unslinging his machine-pistol. "I've allus wanted to kill me a spaghetti-eater. *Mani in alto*," he cried in bad Italian, jerking the muzzle of his weapon upwards in a threatening manner.

Instantly Pitman went into his terrified Eyetie act. He let his shoulders slump. His bottom lip quivered. He contorted his face and raised his hands in the classic pose of supplication. "*Nix schiessen*," he pleaded in broken German, looking as if he might break into tears at any moment.

"Get a gander at that, Otto," the other para sneered. "He's gonna cream his skivvies in half a mo."

"I'm gonna cream *him*, you mean," the ugly one retorted and clicked off his safety.

Pitman's brain raced frantically. It was one of those moments at war which happened all too often. Soldiers wandering off on the line, looking for some mischief – rape, booze, loot – and, brutalised as they were, suddenly stumbling on an unexpected victim, with whom they could toy at their leisure before killing him like they might some stray cat. "Christ," he whispered to himself, "to die like this!"

But Major Pitman was not fated to die – not just yet at least.

As the bigger of the two drunken paras jerked up the muzzle of his machine-pistol to indicate that he should raise his hands even further, the binoculars which he had concealed underneath his loose tunic slipped from their hiding place and tumbled to the hot dusty earth of the field.

Drunk as they were, the two of them were on to it like a shot. "Field glasses!" the bigger one hissed as if he had made a tremendous discovery.

Pitman's heart skipped a beat. He clenched his fists. He was going tamely, to a slug behind his right ear in the usual *coup de grâce* without a fight. That wasn't to be. For the other para exclaimed, "*Spion*, Otto. The spaghetti-eater's a frigging spy . . ."

Otto reacted at once. "The treacherous bastard," he yelled in a sudden blind rage and lashed out. The muzzle of the machine-pistol caught Pitman completely by surprise as it slammed into the pit of his stomach. He groaned and doubled up with pain, face contorted, hands grabbing instinctively for his belly. Otto brought the butt of the weapon down hard on the base of his skull. He gave one solitary yelp of pain and then he was falling, red and white stars exploding in front of his eyes. He was out to the world even before he struck the hot, dusty earth . . .

Mr Yates and Colonel Pitman

Yates was in a savage mood.

He glowered through the great window at the hills beyond on the German frontier. Heavy leaden-grey clouds were assembling above them, indicating that there was snow on the way. Apparently, from what the old chap below had told him, the snow always came early to this part of the world. That's why it was called the 'Snow Eifel'.

It had all started with the girl in bed. He had laid on a skinful just before she had slipped into his bedroom the previous night as he thought it would put him in the right playful mood for the kind of fun and games she liked. It hadn't. She'd not been in the mood at all. Instead she had lain motionless and stared at the ceiling.

Drink and anger had gone to his head and he soon subsided into a drunken sleep.

That hadn't been all. The next morning, his head throbbing, dark circles under his eyes, he had gone down for one of his host's early breakfasts, but to his surprise the Colonel hadn't been there. Shivering in the bare hall, he had asked the servant with the green baize apron where the Colonel was, to be told that "The master isn't feeling too well this morning, sir. He's taking breakfast in his bedroom." The servant had barely looked at him, as if he already knew all about the previous night.

"But he promised—" Yates had begun, realising that today was his last opportunity to get something out of the cynical old man. He controlled his anger swiftly; he knew it would get him nowhere. So he had smiled and asked, "Will the Colonel be available later?"

The servant had still not looked at him. He had continued

polishing the silver plate and had answered, *"I don't doubt he'll see you for dinner, seeing that you are departing tomorrow."* The way that the servant had emphasised the 'departing' had made him look sharply at the Belgian, but his face had revealed nothing. And with that he had been forced to be content.

Now Yates stared at the ever-growing snow clouds, wondering how he should proceed. He knew Jenkins boasted he was *'a hire-and-fire man par excellence. Produce or you're out on yer lughole.'* Jenkins would have no compunction about firing him if he came back from Belgium without a story. But how could he get a story out of that hard bastard, the Colonel? Twice in the last couple of days he thought that Pitman had been ready to come across. But in the last minute he had pulled back so that he knew now that Pitman had been playing him along all the time.

But then these old guys of the Establishment, with their old school ties, clubs, connections, were all like that. Everyone thought their breed had long died out, but they hadn't – and if they had, they had been replaced by another bunch of chinless wonders.

He puffed angrily at his tenth cigarette of the morning, though his quack had warned him against too much drinking and smoking. *"Damn him, too,"* he whispered under his breath at the memory. *"So I die a year earlier. So what!"*

It was in that kind of a mood that the newspaperman, with sharp nose and narrow eyes so that he looked a little like the fox he was, wandered out of the big house – silent save for the persistent creaks of the ancient woodwork – down the icy fields towards the little stream which marked the border between Belgium and Germany. As he walked his anger started to change to determination. Why should he let the old man get the better of him? The Colonel would *be dead in a year or so;* he *had years to go and he had to earn his keep for those years to come. Why should Pitman go to his grave taking his precious secrets with him, lost to the world for ever – and whatever money that could be made with those secrets? After all, he ought to make ten grand out of it at least.*

No! *He couldn't let Pitman off the hook. He'd have to be as persistent, as tough and as aggressive as the old boy. What was it some old general had once said? 'The best defence is attack.'*

He stopped at the little border stream, ice patches already beginning to form at its banks. On the opposite side, under the shelter of what looked like a wall of rough shale, he could see the regular line of shallow holes, with in their middle a square-shaped one, walls of earth, now long moss-covered, around it, from which protruded strands of khaki-coloured wire. For a few moments he stared at the line in bewilderment, wondering what it was, while the little stream bubbled and chuckled its way merrily into Germany beyond.

Then he had it. It was a line of foxholes from some long-forgotten skirmish of the old war. Once young men had lain in those holes, fearful or elated, waiting for the enemy to come to be killed or for they themselves to be killed. That had been over half a century ago, he told himself. Who cared about their fate now? Those who had survived were very old men now, living off their memories – That is, if the bloody Alzheimer's hasn't got 'em, *a cynical little voice commented at the back of his head.*

The thought reinforced his determination to have a real go at the ancient Colonel. He'd had his day. He was history – ancient *history. The present belonged to him, not to some ancient relic, just waiting around to snuff it. He smiled at himself in the wavering reflection in the water. As the first sad flakes of snow started to drift down, heralding what was to come, he turned and began to ascend the hill to the village and chateau beyond. He was filled with renewed confidence. There'd be no more pussyfooting about. This time he'd get what he wanted –* or else!

Muffled in a plaid rug, his 'mixture' at his side, Colonel Pitman watched him come. He could have guessed what the newspaperman was thinking. People of his generation, he thought scornfully, always wore their hearts on their sleeves. They behaved spontaneously, however outrageously, any way they wanted. They said, without thinking, the first thing that came into their minds. They weren't like the English of his own time, who played the game with their cards close to their chests, revealing little. That's why they survived. He pursed his thin, bloodless, somewhat cruel lips. Yes, that's why they survived while people like Mr Yates were fated to die young – as he would.

He took a careful sip at his 'mixture', savouring the burn but careful not to drink enough to make himself cough. For a moment or two he heard the old tunes of glory – the crisp stamp of heavy boots in unison on gravel; the harsh commands; the slap of heavy hands striking rifle butts with precision as the soldiers went through the manual of arms. In a wintry fashion he gave a careful little smile, happy with the memory of a time when there was order and discipline and life had a purpose. Then he dismissed the indulgence and concentrated on what he had to do with Mr bloody Yates.

Yates had drunk too much of the Colonel's whisky, which Pitman had offered him time and time again, as if he were

*not in one little bit offended by the younger man's aggress-
iveness. And with his increasing drunkenness his anger
had grown progressively. Sitting there, the big tumbler
of whisky clutched in both hands, as if he were afraid
he might drop it, with the snow coming down in a solid
white wall outside the big stained-glass window, he glared
red-faced at the old Colonel and snorted,* "Oh come on,
Colonel, grow up. Let's get this done with. If you want
money for your information, I've got a contract in my
bag all ready and waiting. There'll be at least five grand
in it . . . and if we get an American sale, you can reckon
another twenty on top of that." *He took a great gulp of
the neat spirit.* "You'll be able to give yourself a holi-
day, somewhere warm and bright, and away from this
gloomy dump. You deserve it. Well?" *he leaned forward
expectantly.*

*Pitman took his time in the fashion of old men who
weren't going anywhere.* "To be quite frank with you, Mr
Yates, money doesn't interest me and I'm not particularly
interested in somewhere – er – warm and bright."

Yates took another tack. "All right, if you won't play ball
with me, you'll have to with somebody else and you'll go
out of it empty-handed and – my guess is – your reputation
in rags."

*Pitman was unimpressed. He raised his bushy eyebrows
to indicate that Yates should continue, that was all.*

"You must realise," *Yates lectured him now, his speech
slightly slurred, eyes red and angry,* "we live in a global
village, if you know what that means—"

Pitman nodded.

"You can't hide anyone or anything. If I don't get the
information I want, someone else will. So why don't you
stop pussyfooting about? Give me the info and let me get off

to Liège and then back to London tomorrow." He paused, his chest heaving.

Colonel Pitman looked out of the window at the flying snow beating at the leaden panes, and then at Yates, as if he was seeing him for the first time. He told himself that the journalist looked the mongrel runt he was. There was no style about him. His horizon was limited to money and a little transitory fame. Why should he allow himself to be blackmailed by a shit like Yates? Why should he permit the Great Man's name to be dragged through the mud in order that he and his equally cheap bosses should sell a few more thousand copies of their gutter rag? He decided to call the now obviously drunken Yates's bluff. He took a sip at the 'mixture' to fortify himself and said, "I'm afraid I can't help you, Mr Yates."

Yates looked at him with his burning, drunken gaze. "Can't?" he exploded. "You mean you won't."

Pitman shrugged his shoulders slightly. "Yes, if you want to put it like that," he replied.

"And who the fuck ever told you you could do what you like, Colonel?" Yates snarled.

Pitman didn't respond, but his left cheek began to twitch. It was something that Yates, in his overwhelming rage didn't see. He would have desisted there and then if he had, for it was a danger signal. But he overlooked it. By the time he came to think of that sudden nervous tic on the Colonel's face it would be too late.

"You lot with your bloody polished medals, yer regimental ties and all that bull, walking up and down like frigging Jesus across the water – well, all that crap's over. We – no, you – lost the Empire. You can't blame us for that – we were only kids then. And now you can't pay the price. Holy shit, you don't even seem to realise the fact that you have *lost it."* He paused, his unathletic chest heaving with the effort.

"*I take your point, Yates,"* Colonel Pitman said calmly. "*You might be right. But it still doesn't alter the fact that I have a certain attitude and I'm sticking to it – say what you may."*

"*All right then, bugger you,"* Yates cried, besides him with exasperation. He gulped the rest of the drink down in one gulp and slammed the glass down hard on the antique table. "*But remember this – we'll get the Churchill story whatever you think to the contrary. After all,"* he yelled as a parting shot, "*Churchill wasn't so pure. I mean, what do you make of a bloke who was still negotiating with the Eyetie Fascist boss when we were losing thirteen thousand soldiers killed at El Alamein, three years after we'd gone to war with Italy?"* He looked down contemptuously at the stony-faced old man. *That's your high-and-mighty true-blue Tory you're trying to protect, mate."* And with he turned and stormed out.

Colonel Pitman said nothing. For what seemed a long time he sat slumped in his chair, the plaid wrapped tighter around his shoulders to keep out the piercing cold in the poorly heated room. To all the world he might have well been dead already.

Outside the snow beat at the window in a white fury, making the panes rattle, peppering them with snowflakes like pieces of shrapnel. Colonel Pitman didn't seem to notice. He was too wrapped up in his thoughts, with that almost forgotten past in Italy when he and the rest had risked their lives for what the Great Old Man was wont to call the 'King Emperor and his Domain'. Then he forced himself to direct his attention to the present.

He told himself that he had – at the most – thirty-six hours left. Yates thought himself safe. The world he lived in didn't admit of violent sudden death when it was least expected. Yates had still not realised with whom he was dealing: an old man who had grown up in a time when nothing could be taken for granted – save death.

He reached for the house phone to call Molitor, his mind made up, Yates's death warrant already signed.

Part Four

THE SKORZENY PLOT

Chapter Sixteen

Pitman paused and listened. It was the middle of the night, and everyone should be sleeping, including the Italian sentries – they always did, in his experience. But sound carried a long way at night and since the parachute Intelligence officer, Schwarz, had arrived the previous midday he knew he had to be doubly careful.

Unlike the Italian *Teniente*, who had first captured him when the two Germans had handed him over to the *Carabinieri*, Schwarz was a true professional; Pitman could see that all right. Behind his thick hornrims, his eyes were quick and intelligent and he knew from the way he had questioned the other prisoners, mostly Italian deserters, a couple of communist peasants and a handful of British escaped POWs who could be nothing else but Englishmen despite their Italian peasant rags, he knew his business. Besides, he was fluent both in English and Italian and if anyone was going to spot Pitman's unRoman accent, it would be *Oberleutnant* Schwarz.

Hence it was imperative not to draw attention to himself – wasn't he a good loyal Fascist imprisoned by mistake? All the same he had to get out of the pigsty which served as his cell before Schwarz really started interrogating him

He had noticed the 'piss bucket' immediately the MPs had thrown him into the farmyard pigsty which served as

a jail. Naturally he had known that he had to be alone –
he couldn't trust anyone, including the hearty Englishmen,
all sporting the same moustaches which marked them as
escaped POWs at once. He had insisted in Italian that
he couldn't possibly, as a Fascist officer, be imprisoned
together with the English swine. So while the rest had
been shoved into the cowshed, he had been incarcerated
in the pigsty, ankle deep in pigshit, by himself. Almost at
once he had started work on the enamel inside of the rusting
bucket, trying to pare off handy-sized lengths of the sharp,
brittle stuff.

It had been hard work and his fingers were already cut
and bleeding, but slowly and surely, he was getting to the
large piece in the middle, made of thicker enamel and the
size of a pocket knife. He didn't know how exactly, but he
reasoned it was the piece with which he'd get out of his
makeshift prison, if at all.

In the heavy silence of the middle of the night, broken only
by the muted snoring and occasional cry of the prisoners in the
bigger cowshed opposite, he worked at the bucket. He was
repulsed by the stench of the waste products of generations
of Italian peasants, which would be used for manuring the
fields in the spring. Time and time again the sharp, brittle
edge of the enamel sliced into his fingers and the sides of
the bucket – if he could have seen them – would have been
red with his own blood, he knew. All the same he worked
doggedly at his task, knowing that he must escape before
Oberleutnant Schwarz started to work on him. For then,
after Schwarz had ferreted out the truth, all he could expect
was the thugs of the Gestapo or the Italian *Ovra* and finally
a quick death at the side of the farmhouse's wall.

Time passed leadenly. They had looted his watch and his
wallet so he had no way of judging what the time was,

though he guessed six o'clock would be the time they changed the sentries. Before that there would be the familiar clatter of the cooks making the morning 'drumfire', as they nicknamed their morning coffee laced with *grappa*.

By now his nerves were on edge as he cocked his head constantly to one side to listen for any sound that might be suspicious. His fingertips were bloody rags and he gritted his teeth to stifle the pain every time he attacked the inside of the bucket. But there was no other way. Behind him the pigsty was barred by a heavy iron rusting door. If it had had a lock, it would have been a matter of moments to pick. But it hadn't. Instead it was barred from the outside and there was only one way to get rid of that bar between him and freedom; and that was to remove the rusting screws which held the door to its hinges. If he could get through them, he'd be out to face whatever dangers lay beyond.

Now and again the pigs shuffled, alarmed by the constant movement he was making – but all the same it made him jump every time they did so. He told himself more than once he had to get a grip on himself. It was the only way he was going to get out of this damned place before dawn.

By what he calculated later was four o'clock that morning, with the dirty white light of the false dawn already beginning to creep through the gaps in the ancient stonework of the Italian pigsty, he had broken off two large pieces of the jagged razor-sharp enamel. For a moment or two he nursed his hands, which were aflame with pain. But not for long. He knew he hadn't a minute to waste. As best he could, he wound up the thinner of the two with the sharper point in the stinking straw of the pigsty, then tied it on with the bloodstained rag of his handkerchief.

That done he approached the upper of the two hinges. He hoped that if he could undo the screws on that hinge, it would put so much weight on the lower one that it would sag of its own accord and thus not need unscrewing separately. Narrowing his eyes in the evil-smelling gloom of the place, up to his ankles in pig slime, he wet his right finger and ran it over the two screws to clear them of the muck of generations.

Immediately he could see that they were well rusted into their holes. "Tough," he whispered to himself. "They're going to be tough to undo." Praying that the sharp end of the enamel, which he would use to turn the thread – if he were lucky – wouldn't break off before he completed his task, he commenced his odyssey.

It seemed an age before he could finally clear away the rust and grime so that he could get a hold on the thread of the upper of the two screws. Saying a half-forgotten prayer, he took the strain. Nothing . . . nothing happened!

"Damn," he hissed under his breath and commanded himself not to go beserk. He counted to three and started once again. This time he chanced snapping the point of the brittle metal by inserting it into the far corner of the screw. Nothing happened. He breathed a little sigh of relief. Infinitely slowly, beads of cold sweat standing out on his forehead like pearls, his heart beating furiously, he chanced a first turn. *The screw moved!*

He could have shouted aloud with triumph, but he didn't. It had taken him a good five minutes, he reasoned, to get this far. He'd need every minute he could find without advertising what he was doing to the Italian guards outside. Carefully he applied the pressure once more. Again the screw moved and by dint of peering hard in the malodorous gloom, he could see the metal below glint. The thread was whole and not corroded by rust. He said a silent prayer of thanks.

He worked steadily and carefully, taking out the first screw. Finally it was done and he rested his burning hands for a few moments, staring at the hole where the screw had been in triumph, as if he had created something of great value. A creak, followed by the gush of someone urinating into a bucket similar to his own alerted him to the danger. Someone could come in at any time and they wouldn't need a crystal ball to realise what he was about. He'd be in trouble – serious trouble – in double-quick time.

He commenced working on the second screw. Again it seemed to take an age before he got the thread moving, the enamel edge of the makeshift knife cracking alarmingly as he did so. "Come on – last," he commanded it. "Please – *last*!"

Minutes ticked by. Outside there was no sound again save for the snorts of the uneasy animals. Whoever had urinated had gone back to sleep once more. With his fingers bleeding hard now, but the pain reduced for some reason he couldn't quite fathom, he eased the screw out of the hole bit by bit, each turn of the thread a major achievement. His whole being was concentrated on the screw. It seemed as if he had known no other life than this, working, working, working at the reluctant screw.

Suddenly he was startled by the movement of the heavy, ancient door. For a fleeting second he couldn't understand what had happened. Then as the screw started to buckle and he began unwinding the last few threads before the metal pin buckled irretrivably into the hole in the woodwork, the door started to sag. The pressure was off the top hinge and was being transferred to the lower one.

"*Out!*" he hissed, and inserting his bloody hand through the new gap, caught hold of the door just before it sagged beyond redemption. For what seemed an eternity he did not dare move, frozen in a ghastly tableau. Then slowly, infinitely slowly, he commenced the next movement, heart beating like a trip-hammer.

Exerting the last of his strength, he raised the heavy door and wedged the toecap of his right boot underneath it so that it could not sag and buckle. Now his movements seemed like those of an old and very feeble man. But he was not taking any chances that a hasty sudden movement might spoil the whole business at this late stage; for he knew that dawn was approaching. Far off at some other farm he could hear the first crows of triumph of some proud cock, well pleased with his amatory progress.

It was all nip and tuck, so much so that a sweating Pitman hardly dared breathe at times, as he tried to manoeuvre the door and the bar on the other side of the gap he had forced by undoing the hinges. One false move and he would lose control of the situation, and then he might as well resign himself to the firing squad and that final pistol shot to the nape of his neck.

Sweating all over, gasping for breath, he wriggled his fingers forward bit by bit in order to wedge them underneath the retaining bar that kept him prisoner in the pigsty. The weight of the door on his toes seemed to grow more intolerable by the second. He dug his teeth into his bottom lip until the blood came. He couldn't give in now – *he couldn't*!

Suddenly his forefinger slipped under the bar. He gasped with relief. He had it! For a few moments he paused, trying to control the trembling of his hand before he took the next step. Outside someone mumbled something in his sleep, and there was the creak of straw as he turned over. Again Pitman was amazed at the distances noise travelled at night. Then he concentrated on the final task before he was free.

Gingerly, forcing himself to take his time, he started to raise the bar and then draw it backwards so that it would come off the catch outside which held it. He seemed to take a devil of a lot of time to do so and the bar squeaked rustily as he did. Christ, he cursed to himself, they'll hear this in Rome.

But whoever 'they' were didn't. Slowly but surely, the bar came out from its restraint. Inch by inch he pulled the bar backwards, hardly daring to breathe, his ears atuned to the slightest unusual sound. But there was none. He was getting away with it. The Gestapo or the Italian secret police, the *Ovra*, would not get their dirty paws on him after all.

Finally he had done it. He tested the door gingerly. It started to open slowly. He paused and collected himself. He would need all his wits about him for the next few moments before he cleared this makeshift prison out in the middle of nowhere. Hastily he bent, undid his bootlaces, took off his holed sweaty socks, replaced the boots on his naked feet and drew the socks on afterwards. It was an old trick, but it would give him the advantage in a military environment in which everyone clumped round in noisy heavy Army boots. He should be almost noiseless.

Now he was ready. He moved the door inch by inch. Somewhere outside the cattle shuffled uneasily and breathed out hard. He could smell their warm milky scent. But the sounds didn't worry him. He was used to them now and besides, the guards, if they were disturbed by them, would associate them with the usual noises of a pre-milking farmyard. Heifers didn't get impatient about now.

He started to make his way through the gloomy beflagged passage, peering for cowpats in the darkness. He didn't want to slip on one and make a racket falling. He was carrying the other piece of razor-sharp enamel. It would serve as a dagger, unless he thrust it forward at anyone trying to stop him in the wrong way and the blade broke off on impact.

But he told himself it wasn't going to come to that. All was quiet. The farm remained silent. His progress quickened. He was nearly out of the makeshift jail now. He could feel the cooler dawn air fan about his flushed face. Someone had left a door open. He passed a room of snoring men, mumbling in their sleep, their straw mattresses squeaking audibly as they turned.

Then suddenly, joyously, he was out in the muddy farmyard, breathing in the fresh air of freedom in great heady gulps. Beyond lay the endless fields of maize, dripping a little with the dawn dew. Once in there, he told himself confidently, they'd never catch him again. It would give him the cover he needed till he reached the Alban hills, where he would attempt to make contact with one of the SOE rescue teams now stationed in newly conquered Sicily.

He jumped. Not more than ten yards away someone had given a low moan, not of pain, but of pleasure. It was followed by a male voice whispering gruffly in German, "Don't worry, little cheetah, it won't hurt. Now try that on again for collar size."

"Bloody hell," he cursed to himself. "Someone's out there – at this time of the morning as well."

They certainly were.

In the same instant that he saw them, the girl, some milkmaid perhaps, saw him. She cried out. The soldier, a guard possibly, busy lowering his pants to his ankles in preparation, swung round and saw the shadowy figure standing there.

"*Verdammtes Schwein*," he called in rage and lunged out.

161

Pitman thrust his crude knife forward instinctively. He heard it drive into the man's naked belly with a dreadful noise. The man stared at him, fists turned to claws, as if he could not believe that this was happening to him. He grabbed Pitman by the jacket while the girl started to scream in Italian. Pitman thrust the knife in deeper. Still the German didn't let go. "For Chrissake," he heard himself scream desperately – and he would hear that scream in his nightmares for many years to come – "Die . . . *DIE!*"

But still the German refused to do so as the hot blood streamed up Pitman's fingers and onto his taut wrist. Besides himself with rage and panic, as he heard the soldiers inside begin to stir with cries of *"What's going on . . . Who's making the racket out there . . . Like a stuck pig . . ."* he thrust home the makeshift knife yet once again. He heard it glance off a bone sickeningly and break off. The soldier's spine arched like a taut bow. Pitman pulled at his jacket. But in the rictus of death the German held on to it, as if – even at this final moment of his young life – it was the most precious thing in the world to him.

Pitman wriggled free, his breath coming in great broken-hearted sobs. The Italian girl, legs still spread, continued to scream in a piercing manner which cut through him like a sharp knife. He could stand it no longer. He had to get away from this bloodbath. Leaving the dying German still hanging on to his jacket, he staggered, sobbing and mumbling to himself like a man demented, towards the maize field.

A challenge. A curse. Angry scarlet flame stabbed the morning gloom. A bullet thwacked through the heads of maize. He awoke to the imminent danger. He got a hold of himself. Bent low, going all out in a crazy zig-zag, he began running through the maize, the big rough heads lashing his sweat-lathered, crazed face like whips. It didn't matter. He didn't feel them. All he knew was that he had to get away . . .

Chapter Seventeen

The newly appointed *Obersturmbannführer* was drunk, happy and virtually naked. But then he had been in that state for most of the time since he made his triumphant arrival back in Vienna together with *il Duce* five days before. It had been honour after honour; party after party. Never before and never again would he experience such delights and such honours. Why, even that drunken old sot Churchill had praised his rescue in the English Houses of Parliament – honour indeed!

Just before he had left to meet the Führer in Berlin, Mussolini had kissed him on both cheeks in the Italian fashion and then to Skorzeny's surprise had handed him a silver wristwatch, encrusted with jewels and inscribed, *'To My Rescuer'*. It had been a splendid, expensive present and in years to come, whenever the Austrian was asked the time, he would flash the wristwatch and ask mysteriously, "Would you like Mussolini time?"

It had been the first of many presents. The next night, when Skorzeny had been attempting to soak in the great marble tub once used by the Austrian Emperor, Franz Josef himself, *helped* by two native Viennese girls, a flustered, red-faced Colonel of the Greater German General Staff had been ushered into the bathroom, all polished high boots and creaking corsetted waist. The Colonel had wiped the steam from his monocle and, trying to keep his eyes off the girls' plump, rose-tipped breasts, announced: "In the name of the Führer, I am empowered to bestow on your person on behalf of a grateful German Nation the Knight's Cross of the Iron Cross . . . By proxy, of course," he had added when Skorzeny had looked puzzled. Thereupon he had unclipped the Knight's Cross from his own neck and placed it upon Skorzeny's. He had left hastily, gaze on the floor, to the giggles of the girls and Skorzeny's great drunken, "In three devils' name, I bet I'm the first German soldier to cure his throatache, drunk in a bath, attended," he had rolled his eyes suggestively, "by two such charming ladies."

So it had gone. Telegrams from high and low had poured in. Himmler had signalled he was to be promoted to *Obersturmbannführer* immediately. 'Fat Hermann', as Hermann Goering, the enormous head of the *Luftwaffe* was known behind his back, had hinted over the phone that there might well be a general's post opened to him if he decided to transfer to the *Luftwaffe*. 'The Poisoned Dwarf' naturally wasn't prepared to to be left out either. Dr Goebbels had stated quite openly that he could use Skorzeny urgently, If he, Skorzeny, would undertake a propaganda tour of the occupied and allied countries, he would ensure he would sleep with some of the best-known film actresses in Europe – and he mentioned names which made Skorzeny's eyes pop – and that, in return, too, a full-length feature film might well be made of his dramatic rescue of the Duce.

So Skorzeny, still in Vienna enjoying the honours, the pleasures and the women, many of them high-born, who were absolutely throwing themselves at him, was not surprised when the hotel reception announced that *Oberleutnant* Schwarz, who apparently had escorted the Duce's family out of Italy to their new home in Bavaria, courtesy of the Führer, would like to see him urgently. At first Skorzeny, still very drunk from the enormous amounts of French champagne he had consumed in the Palais of a Viennese countess, who had done things for him he had hardly believed possible, was inclined to say no. But when the receptionist had added, *"G'nädiger Herr, der Herr Doktor Oberleutnant* says it is *very, very* important," he relented. He knew his Austrians. When they started throwing around titles such as '*Herr Doktor*' it meant they were very impressed. He ordered the receptionist to send him up while he bathed his head hurriedly in a sinkful of ice-cold water.

Schwarz, smart and well turned out, but obviously no soldier, looked indeed like a *Herr Doktor*, a former high school professor before the War, very correct and polite, save for his dark, cunning eyes and the cowl of close-cropped blond hair coming to a widow's peak low on his forehead, so that it looked almost as if the *Luftwaffe* officer was wearing a medieval peaked skull cap. Still, drunk as he was, Skorzeny was impressed and not a little afraid. There was something very sinister about *Herr Oberleutnant* Schwarz.

For a few moments while Schwarz sipped his vintage Tokay like a maiden aunt afraid that a man was about to take advantage of her virtue – Skorzeny asked the usual questions. One day soon, he would not have to undergo this ritual, he knew. Important people never did. But for the time being he was content to appear less important than he was. Finally he remembered he had a date with a young actress at the *Burgtheater* later that afternoon and that he didn't have all the time in the world for lowly *Oberleutnants* doomed to obscurity. So he said, 'Well, Schwarz, I'm sure you don't want to waste your valuable home leave time telling me these somewhat mundane details of the Duce's family. Where's the fire?" The question came out hard and almost challenging.

Schwarz showed no surprise. Those calculating eyes remained wary. He said, "I don't know exactly, *Obersturmbannfuhrer*" – that impressed Skorzeny; the man already knew he had been promoted when no one else in Vienna did – "if there's a fire, but I think that we have the start of one."

Skorzeny looked puzzled. "I don't understand, Schwarz," he stuttered.

"Let me then explain," the other man said, as if he were dealing with a not-too-bright schoolboy. "The same night that you flew away to the *Ostmark*" – he used the Nazi name for Austria, which Skorzeny didn't like. He sensed instinctively that Schwartz had used it deliberately. Was he trying to take a rise out of him? – "we took a prisoner. He was dressed in Italian uniform, spoke fluent Italian, and German too for that matter." He paused as if to make sure Skorzeny was taking it all in. "But I, personally, think he was an Englishman."

"An Englishman?" Skorzeny echoed, surprised in spite of himself. "What would a Tommy be doing in the middle of all that high-level business?"

Schwarz pursed his lips. For what seemed a long time he didn't say anything. Outside Skorzeny could hear the familiar ring of the bells of the blue-painted trams. Further away a brass band was playing a gay Austrian march of the turn of the century – more like a dance tune played in the wine gardens of Grinzing than the solemn blare of brass of the *Wehrmacht* bands. He was aware of a pleasant feeling. There was no fame to be gained in the old Imperial city – time had passed it – but it was a perfect place to live and love.

"Espionage." Schwarz finally broke his silence.

"*Espionage?*"

"*Jawohl, Obersturmbannführer.* You heard correctly."

"But what was he trying to do? So he was there in Mussolini's area. But what could he do about it?" Skorzeny objected, puzzled. "One man, when we had a whole parachute division *and* an armoured regiment, Wotan, under command. How could this Englishman of yours rescue Mussolini under those circumstances?"

By way of an answer, Schwarz took what looked like a battered wallet from his immaculate briefcase. As he did so Skorzeny told himself the man was a pedant, but a clever and dangerous one. There was no denying that.

"The wallet taken from the Englishman just before he killed one of my people and escaped. At first sight," – he turned the wallet round like a magician about to play some trick or other it – "it seems perfectly, you'll agree, *Obersturmbannführer*, harmless. But it isn't." Before Skorzeny could comment, he pressed some sort of button. As if by magic a side pocket which Skorzeny hadn't seen up to then, opened.

Schwarz gave a tight little smile, pleased that he had surprised the hero of the hour. He took a small sliver of paper out of the secret compartment and without handing it to Skorzeny, as if he were afraid the latter might lose or damage it, said, "A special number in the Vatican—"

"Vatican?" Skorzeny echoed in surprise.

"Yes, it's from their college there that the English run their spy ring in Italy." Schwarz shrugged carelessly, as if he were wasting precious time explaining such obvious things to his listener. "The number is an emergency one to be used by the English spies only in dire emergencies. The fugitive has used it."

"And?" Skorzeny asked urgently, intrigued now by Schwarz's report, the actress from the Burgtheater momentarily forgotten.

"Our agent reported he was turned down until—" Schwarz hesitated in a slightly dramatic way for him, as if he wished to get the fullest value from his surprise.

"Go on?"

"He mentioned the English Prime Minister, Churchill."

"*Churchill!*" Skorzeny echoed, taken completely by surprise.

"Yes – Churchill and the 'key papers'. Those are the exact words, according to our agent."

If Schwarz had expected Skorzeny to be taken by surprise at the mention of the Churchill 'papers', he was in for a disappointment. For the Austrian was already visualising that scene in the hotel on the Gran Sasso when Mussolini had been more concerned with his briefcase, stuffed with papers, than the fact he had to get off the mountain as soon as possible. Even then he had wondered at the great importance the prisoner had attached to them.

Instead Skorzeny said thoughtfully, "If the Tommies were prepared to send such a high-level agent to the Gran Sasso – and he must have been important, the way their lot in the Vatican reacted – then there must have been something in the 'Churchill Papers', as we'll call them, of the greatest significance. But what?" His voice trailed away and he frowned with frustration, for Skorzeny was not a thinking man, but one of action.

Outside a battalion was marching to the station, probably off to the front in Russia, singing lustily about the 'nut-brown maiden' they were leaving behind them, while a drunk was heckling them.

But neither Skorzeny nor *Oberleutnant* Schwarz were

aware of the events taking place in the street outside; they were concentrating too hard on the problem at hand.

Finally Schwarz broke the taut silence. He reached into the leather officers' satchel attached to his gleaming uniform belt and took out a buff-coloured flimsy, saying, "I am a rather low-ranking intelligence officer, *Obersturmbannführer*. But I have friends in somewhat higher places, who sometimes supply me with information when they think it might be useful to me or of interest."

Skorzeny looked at him as if he were seeing the ex-teacher for the very first time. He realised that Schwarz was not only intelligent, but devious. How else could an ordinary intelligence officer, presumably engaged in routine interrogations of prisoners of war and the like have the ear of someone on the Berlin Greater German General Staff? But he made nothing of it. Instead he said, "What is it?" Already he had become used to the habits of the great and famous, who never read anything themselves but let their underlings do it for them.

Schwarz wasted no time. "I shall give you a summary, *Obersturmbannführer*," he snapped. "Most of these official signals, especially from Intelligence, are gobbledegook pure and simple." He glanced at the flimsy momentarily. "It is a report from our *Abwehr* – Secret Service – agents in Spain. They report that Churchill has employed a secret slush fund of two million pounds to subvert, by bribery, leading figures in Franco's Spain."

"Go on," Skorzeny urged without too much interest, wondering where all this was leading, unaware that in a few short years those same bribed Falangists would be saving his skin when he was on the run from the Allied forces.

"According to our *Abwehr* people, that money is being used by Churchill to bribe leading civilian and military advisers to the *Caudillo*" – Franco, the Spanish leader – "not to join the War on Germany's side." Schwarz's clever face lit up. "It is an ingenious example of Churchill's manner of securing influence, *Obersturmbannführer*."

Skorzeny agreed. "But what has this got to do with our problem?" he asked, slightly confused by this latest piece of information.

"This, sir," Schwarz snapped, as if he had been waiting all along for the SS officer to ask him that question. "Let us say that that bag contains details of contacts between Mussolini and Churchill about leading Italian politicians, even the King himself, who soon the British will have to accept into the Allied camp as true democrats all the time." He laughed cynically at the thought. "And say that Mussolini intends at some time or the other to do a Ciano—"

"A Ciano?" Skorzeny interrupted firmly.

"Yessir. Ciano's secret diaries kept during his time as Italy's foreign secretary are already safely in Switzerland, sir. And as Mussolini's son-in-law and long-time foreign secretary, Ciano knows where all the secrets and where the skeletons are kept. Not only in Italy, sir," Schwarz hinted darkly, "but also here in the Reich."

"But to what purpose?" Skorzeny objected.

"To be used as blackmail, *Obersturmbannführer* . . . to save his fortune, and," the Intelligence officer added sombrely, "in the end, probably his treacherous neck."

Outside all was silent. Vienna, the last gay capital in Europe, was finally going to sleep. Momentarily Skorzeny thought of the buxom little actress from the Burgtheater, who was well worth a sin or two, then he dismissed her. He could see that if Schwarz was correct, he was onto something big here – if he played his cards right. "So you think that

Mussolini has a similar insurance – and that's why this unknown top English agent was involved?"

"I do, sir."

Skorzeny reacted with remarkable speed for him, as the ploy formed almost instantly in his mind. "Schwarz," he rasped.

"Sir?"

"How would you like to transfer to the SS – I can arrange it – in particular to the Hunting Commando Skorzeny?"

Schwarz, for once, was caught off guard. "I . . . I . . ." he stuttered, "don't think I'd be the type for your SS commandos, *Obersturmbannführer*."

"You wouldn't have to be – nothing physical. You'd come under my command only nominally."

"How do you mean, sir?"

"It is pretty obvious that everything is in a turmoil in Italy. Revolution and betrayal are in the air. The left hand does know what the right is doing. Fascists of twenty years' standing have betrayed their leader, the Duce, to the King and the plotters around him. If they had their way – to save their own rotten, treacherous skins – they'd betray him to the Western Allies as well. That's why Mussolini is hanging on to those documents – the Churchill Papers – whatever they contain. In essence the only people that the Duce can trust are us, the Germans, in particular, yours truly," he poked a thumb at his broad chest, "the man who rescued him. Now," Skorzeny continued, "I am going to suggest to the Führer when I see him in Berlin that Hunting Commando Skorzeny provide a permanent and special bodyguard for Mussolini. Just like Lenin after the Revolution, when no one in Russia could be trusted, hired a bodyguard of Lettish mercenaries, who swore a personal oath to the Reds – we shall provide a similar unit, with no ties to the macaronis, whatever their political leanings. Understand?"

Hastily Schwarz nodded he did, but still he was puzzled by the direction of this late-night conversation in the heart of a sleeping Vienna.

"Now, Schwarz, you would be the head of that bodyguard and my personal representative to Mussolini, with the responsibility of protecting him at all times." Skorzeny's scarred face twisted into a crooked, cynical grin. "Naturally, you'll report to me everything that goes on there – you speak the lingo. More importantly, you'll guard those papers – the Churchill Papers – and in the case of an emergency see that they do not disappear with the Duce, but come to me."

"But why, sir, and what use would they be in such a situation?"

Skorzeny didn't answer his questions directly. Instead he said thoughtfully, closing his right eye in a conspiratorial wink, "My dear Schwarz, knowledge is power and I, for one, intend to use that power." He lowered his voice as if he were afraid that somone might be listening outside the old-fashioned double door of the apartment. "I – *you* – will survive this war, Schwarz, and the reason we will survive is that we have taken precautions well in advance to ensure that we possess the weapons, whatever they might be, necessary for survival. So if you agree, Schwarz, this is what I intend you do . . ."

Outside, the lone drunk had come to life again and was now staggering along the empty night streets of the old capital bellowing, "*Wien . . . Wien nur du allein . . . Stadt meiner Träume . . .*"

Even as he explained his plan to a Schwarz suddenly grave-faced and attentive as he realised what the Austrian was proposing, Skorzeny's face contorted cynically. "*Träume* – dreams!" the harsh little voice at the back of his mind rasped contemptuously. "What rubbish. Dreams are for fools . . . *Deeds are the only certainties . . .*"

Chapter Eighteen

Five hundred miles away, SS Assault Regiment Wotan was in position. In the dunes and, further back in the white foothills, staring over the Mediterranean, they waited tensely, each man's finger cocked around the trigger of his weapon. All were wrapped in a cocoon of their own apprehensions and fears, for even the thickest of the Wotan troopers knew that soon the moment of truth would be upon them. Out in the bay, dark, dangerous silhouettes against the lighter night sky, the American fleet had anchored, soon to discharge their deadly cargo. This night the Americans were going to land in mainland Europe. In a matter of hours, the fate of Hitler's vaunted *Festung Europa* would hang in the balance and they all knew it.

"Rotten buggers," Schulze groaned *sotto voce* to von Dodenburg, standing surveying the scene of imminent mayhem in the turret of the command Tiger. "Why can't they stay in their own backyard? Sticking their big Yankee hooters in like that. 'Tain't fair."

"Did you ever think war was?" von Dodenburg said softly, as if to himself.

Over at the invasion fleet Aldis lamps were beginning to wink their urgent messages. Here and there a green signal flare sailed into the night sky to explode with a soft plop and colour all below momentarily in its garish, unreal light.

Faintly the waiting men could hear the rattle of chains and windlasses as boats began to be lowered down the sides of the troopers. By straining hard they thought they could hear the nervous voices of the invaders.

"What's the drill?" Schulze asked apropos of nothing. He knew the drill well enough, von Dodenburg knew that. He was asking the question solely for the benefit of the 'greenhorns', the replacements who had just arrived from the Reich to make up for the grievous losses Wotan had suffered in Russia. He wanted them to think this was little more than a routine exercise – a drill, conducted by umpires, who at the end of the day would bring back the dead, revive the wounded and send them back to barracks for a good hot meal of giddiup – horsemeat – soup and sausage. All a matter of routine, in which no one got hurt.

"Drill?" von Dodenburg told himself he wouldn't know what to do without old hares as Matz and Schulze. "Put a bomb under 'em and tell 'em to go home to America – we don't want to play with 'em no more."

Anything else he might have added was drowned by a great hissing sound, like a huge primeval monster drawing in the first fiery breath before striking. Along the whole horizon, monstrous blast furnaces opened their doors. Cherry red flames erupted on all sides. "For what we are about to receive," von Dodenburg yelled and crossed himself, "let the Good Lord make us truly thankful."

"Amen to that!" Matz yelled and then the terrible barrage descended upon them.

Von Dodenburg's reply was drowned by the angry screech of a hundred great shells streaking through the night sky to the German positions. Immediately all hell was let loose. Fountains of sand and earth were flung high into the air. Great holes appeared in the ground to the defenders' front as if by magic. The air stank of explosive and burnt cordite. The fury and fierceness of the sudden bombardment was inhuman. Men screamed, grasping at their throats as if they were choking, as the air was driven from their lungs. Others sprang from their foxholes, eyes white, wide and crazed, as if they had suddenly been turned mad. A few screamed at the ships, shaking their fists, shrieking for them to stop. A couple, throwing away their rifles, started to bolt to the rear on legs that felt like jelly until NCOs tackled them and wrestled them to the ground, or officers like the Vulture raised their pistols and shot them dead in mid-stride as an example to the others.

Suddenly, as surprisingly as it had started, the bombardment ceased, leaving a loud silence which echoed and re-echoed around the circle of low hills, leaving the defenders dazed and confused, hardly aware of the scores of boat engines chugging away and bringing the invaders through the wave-combed shallows to land in Europe.

"Stand to . . . stand to everywhere!" the officers and NCOs bellowed, popping up out of their foxholes like ghosts risen from the dead. *"Here they come!"*

Everywhere in von Dodenburg's section of the beach, men obeyed the orders, shaking the sand out of their rifles, working the mechanism once or twice to check that it was functioning. On the tanks, the gunners turned their great ponderous turrets, with their deadly overhanging cannon, to face the attack, and von Dodenburg, straining his eyes to catch the first glimpse of the attackers' boats, yelled, "Don't fire until I give the word!"

Schulze repeated the order at a bellow, adding, "And anyone disobeying the CO's order will have me to deal with."

That did it. The men, veterans and greenbeaks, settled down and waited for the slaughter to commence.

On his turret, von Dodenburg watched, now able to make out the first wave of attackers, their boats formed in a white-crested V, chug-chugging to their doom, as if this was simply a military exercise back in their own remote homeland, five thousand kilometres away. They were green, very green, he realised. They'd ceased the covering barrage much too early.

Hardly had he finished the thought then their *jabos* came screaming in at four hundred kilometres an hour. Angry purple flame crackled the length of their gleaming silver wings as they zoomed across the surface of the sea. Vicious red and white tracer threw up the sand of the landing beach in angry spurts. Here and there a Wotan trooper went down, arms flailing, screaming at the unfeeling heavens which had allowed this terrible thing to happen to them. A *jabo* screamed across von Dodenburg's Tiger at surface height. Schulze didn't hesitate. "Try this on for collar size," he snorted angrily, pressing the trigger of the turret machine-gun. Lead spurted upwards. At that range Schulze couldn't miss. The cruel salvo ran the length of the fighter-bomber's blue-painted belly. Metal started to fall in a deadly rain. Desperately the pilot fought to control the stricken plane. To no avail. Suddenly its beak of a nose tipped alarmingly. The pilot wrenched at the shattered controls. They didn't respond. Next moment he slammed into the dunes. With a great roar, in the same instant that the rest of the flight veered to seaward, thinking their job done, the plane exploded. Hastily Schulze and von Dodenburg ducked as pieces of metal – and human body – came raining down on the turret. "Puts yer right off yer fodder," Schulze yelled above the racket unfeelingly. "No consideration, some people."

Von Dodenburg didn't respond. He couldn't. He wanted to vomit.

The first of the anti-personnel mines close to the edge of the beach exploded. It was followed by another – and yet another. Screams rang out everywhere in the lurid darkness as the Americans ran into the line of mines, which Wotan had laid more as a warning than a defensive measure. For a moment von Dodenburg told himself that the *Amis* had gone to ground; then they could mop them up at their leisure as soon as dawn came. But that wasn't to be. Their officers and NCOs would stand no bogging down. They cried, raged, threatened and the assault infantry began to plod forward once more through the heavy wet sand, bodies bent like ancient farmworkers after a hard day's work in the field heading home against a high wind.

The time for retaliation had come. Hurriedly von Dodenburg raised his flare pistol. Holding it pointed straight in the merciless sky above, he pressed the trigger. *Plop*! The red flare, followed by a white one, coloured the abruptly upturned faces of the surprised Americans in their glowing, flickering garish light.

It was the signal.

"Fire at will!" Schulze yelled, the rest of his words drowned as the co-axial machine-guns in every turret opened up furiously. Like swarms of angry hornets, the tracer sped to the defenceless Americans. They went down on all sides, cursing, praying, crying for their mothers, great gaps appearing in the front rank. Still the rest came stamping on through the sand, impelled forward by the unreasoning logic of battle – it wouldn't be they who would be hit, but the next guy or the one next to him. The second line withered away in that deadly hail of steel. Now the beach was littered with their dead and dying. Even as he watched tranfixed, von Dodenburg could not but admire their fatalistic courage in advancing without a vestige of cover, knowing that they couldn't live more than a minute.

As abruptly as it had started, the steam went out of the Americans' first attack. A few of them had broken through Wotan's lines, but the rest were flopping down among the dead and dying. Others started to back off, making pathetic attempts to fire at their killers, though von Dodenburg knew it was just show; they couldn't see and their hands trembled too violently to aim accurately.

A few continued in their mad progress towards the SS. A boy, helmetless, eyes wild in the dying light of the flares, came running up to von Dodenburg's position. Schulze raised his machine-pistol. "No," von Dodenburg yelled urgently. "We need prisoners for Intelligence."

"Those nervous Nellies," Schulze sneered. All the same he lowered his Schmeisser and waited for the boy. He ran straight towards the Tiger, his eyes crazy with fear, his hair tousled and stained with blood, his breath coming in short, sharp, painful gasps.

"*Stop!*" Schulze commanded.

In his unreasoning panic, the young GI didn't seem to hear. He blundered on, hands stretched out in front of him like a blind man trying to find his way.

Schulze didn't hesitate. He stretched out a foot. The boy stumbled, tried to save himself, failed and went down on his knees. Schulze slammed the steel-shod butt of his Schmeisser into the boy's neck and he went out like a light.

The boy's flight seemed to symbolise the end of the American attack. The barrage opened up once more. Rocket batteries joined in with the great battleships' huge guns, sending bank after bank of flaming rockets at Wotan's positions. From the enemy aircraft carrier far out in the bay, fighter-bombers started to take off once more, bearing with them their loads of sudden death. Again all was murder, mayhem and chaos.

The SS cowered in their holes, as the ground trembled and shivered beneath them under the impact of that tremendous barrage. Here and there a young trooper couldn't stand it anymore; they went mad. Screaming and dancing in circles like drunken Red Indians, the men played in the front line, abruptly impervious to death, until finally death tired of their crazed antics and put an end to them.

The Vulture's voice came crackling metallically over the ether. "Be on your guard, Kuno," he used von Dodenburg's first name – things had to be serious for him to do that. "As green as they are, I shouldn't be surprised if the *Amis* don't attempt something on our left or right flank. And remember this," he added, as if it was of great significance, "if we don't hold them here, they've got a foothold and then we've got a helluva job on our hands to get rid of them. *Ende.*"

Routinely von Dodenburg echoed the last '*Ende*', knowing that the Vulture was right. Kesselring was using his elite troops, including Wotan, to stop the enemy on the beaches. If they failed, then the advancing Americans, with their technical superiority would be facing third-rate 'German' troops who weren't really German, but Russian renegades, Tartars, Romanians and the like, the scum of Occupied Europe who had joined the *Wehrmacht* for the spoils, but who weren't naturally inclined to fight for the vaunted 'Thousand Year Reich', which had nothing to do with them.

"Keep your eyes skinned, Schulze," he warned. "Pass it on to the others."

"Like peeled tomatoes in a tin, sir," the NCO said cheerfully, though he could see just how worried the 'Old Man' was.

181

Time passed tensely, as the battleships kept up their fire and at regular intervals the *Jabos* took off from the aircraft carrier to bomb the Germans. But so far there had been no sign of a fresh *Ami* land attack. Indeed, apart from an ambulance craft, covered in red crosses, painted white and brilliantly illuminated by spotlights, which had come in to take off the wounded, there had been no further landings on that bloody Italian beach. All the same, von Dodenburg wasn't sanguine. If the *Amis* were not going to attack here, why had they not moved off to another landing beach? They were going to get ashore here and form a bridgehead come what may, he knew that in his bones.

At about four o'clock on that September morning, with the dogs barking hoarsely in the distance, the crowing of cocks, and the cooks rattling their dixies as they preared a hot meal for those in the foxholes before dawn came and made it almost impossible for them to move about without difficulty and danger, the first low throb of motors – many motors – could be heard out to sea somewhere to the the right.

The defenders were alert immediately, all thoughts of sleep and food forgotten. Von Dodenburg flung up his glasses urgently. Others did the same, the turrets of their guns swinging round electrically to face the new threat from the sea. Von Dodenburg gasped, shocked. To the right, the whole sea was covered by the squat outlines of armoured vehicles hurrying for the land and the second round of the uneven battle.

"Amphibious tanks," he yelled urgently, setting the farm dogs off barking furiously. *"Stand to, everywhere. TANKS FROM THE SEA . . . THREE O'CLOCK . . . STAND TO!"*

Chapter Nineteen

At the joint Allied corps fighting the first battle for Italy, all was controlled confusion. In the ancient Palazzo which they had taken over for their battle headquarters, self-important staff officers hurried back and forth, frowning hard, carrying sheafs of paper marked 'top secret' under their arms. Telephones jingled incessantly, as did the clerks' typewriters, cutting new orders for the hard-pressed coastal invaders. Down in the courtyard dispatch-riders, covered in thick white dust, zoomed back and forth. Red Cross jeeps, bearing casualties who had something of importance to report to Intelligence, ground to a halt with their freight of misery.

Up in the ops and maps room, generals yelled at each other angrily. Cigar-smoking one-star generals and brigadiers glanced gloomily at the huge wall map of southern Italy, covered by a rash of red and blue crayon marks which indicated friend and foe, while on the sand table, WACs and ATS pushed the models back and forth with their long wooden pointers.

In the tiny partitioned-off offices to left and right, senior officers spoke loudly into telephones as the teleprinters clacked mercilessly and incessantly, bringing and sending their messages of woe and joy. "Get me Red Beach, for Chrissake," they yelled into the phones, rolling their half-smoked cigars from side to side. *"Where are those 75 mm howitzers . . . our boys are crying blue murder for fire support . . ."* they bellowed, *"I don't give a damn about your casualties, Colonel. You just hold that goddamn hill. If you don't, you can pack your duds and go home to the land of the round doorknob. Got it, Colonel?"* Time and time again they brought their professional, artificial rages into play, cajoling, threatening, bullying, sending ever more reluctant young men to their deaths on that remote beach.

"Total war," Colonel Wintle of the Intelligence Corps, and the secret representative of 'C's SIS at Montgomery's HQ said somewhat cynically. "One wonders sometimes how we can ever win."

"We are *winning*, sir?" Major Pitman queried. He was dressed in rumpled khaki drill with no badges, save his major's pips and the blue and white wings of the operational parachutist on his broad chest. He looked eager – as always – but tired. The last months in Italy, with every man's hand against him, Colonel Wintle told himself, had taken their toil. "Oh yes, we'll win all right. The casualties, especially the Yank ones, have been horrendous. But we've got a toehole in Europe and Clark, who doesn't give a damn about casualties as long as he achieves the glory he's after, is pleased." He referred to the American commander, General Mark Clark, known throughout the Anglo-American armies in the Mediterranean as a poseur, whose main aim in life, it appeared, was to upstage Eisenhower in Britain. "We've turned the flank of these SS Johnnies of that Regiment Wotan; we are advancing – slowly, admittedly – inland. If we can beat their elite, I don't think there's going to be much stopping us."

"I see, sir," Pitman said and watched as a red-faced fat American full colonel 'chewed out' a crestfallen young Major with his right arm in a bloody sling, crying, "I don't give the Sam Hill for your battalion and the casualties, Major. You were expendable from the very start and you'd better believe it. You should have held on."

Miserably the Major opened his mouth to speak, but the Colonel held up his pudgy, beringed hand to stop him. "No excuses, Major. You messed up on the job." He jerked his thumb towards the door guarded by two rigid, immaculate MP sentries. "You're out . . . On your way, buddy."

"So what's the drill now, sir?" Pitman asked as the wounded Major trailed out, shoulders bent in defeat. No one took any notice of him. Now he was one of the invisible men – yesterday's great white hope, today a miserable failure whom no one wanted to know.

"Drill?" the Colonel of Intelligence repeated thoughtfully, as if this was the first time he had given the matter any thought. "Well, Pitman, we might think we're calling the tune now we appear to be winning in Italy, but in reality it's Hitler who's doing that."

"How do you mean, sir?"

"He's going to make us pay a bloody butcher's bill for every foot of Italian earth we gain. He'll fight all the way up the Eyetie boot, battling from one mountain range to the next, abandoning the position when his casualties become greater than ours." The Colonel frowned, as if he had just become aware of the gravity of his statement. "But the closer we get to Rome and the Italian border with the Reich, the more he'll turn the screw. He'll make us pay all right. He needs northern Italy's industrial output for the Reich's war machine and naturally Hitler wants to keep us as far away from the Fatherland as possible."

Pitman absorbed the information but made no comment. Up at the great map, a General was saying gleefully, "We've got him on the run, gentlemen. I know we're paying for it," he didn't even have the soul not to keep smiling at the thought of the casualties this success was costing, "but you can't make an omelette, as the Frogs say, without breaking eggs." He laughed and the rest of the well-nourished, middle-aged officers who would all probably die peacefully in bed, joined in dutifully.

Colonel Wintle sniffed. The patch over his left eye, and his empty right sleeve indicated that he knew only too well the cost of victory. "Brass hats," he commented *sotto voce*. He dismissed the General and continued, "So now Hitler needs his fellow dictator Musso once more. We hear from our secret sources that Hitler is going to establish the former Duce in a puppet republic up in the north in the Lake Garda area. He'll have a proper cabinet, his own army and all the rest of it." He hesitated and Pitman wondered what was coming now, and even as he wondered, he told himself that whatever it was, it would be his own fault.

Immediately after he had been returned to Cairo thanks to the Vatican network, his bosses had offered him a staff job, or return to his newly freed Sicilian estate, anything he wanted but a front-line or clandestine job. Immediately he had asked to be returned to his regiment. They had pointed out his regiment existed no more. It had disappeared into the burning wastes of Africa after the Battle of El Alamein, worn down to nothing in the coastal fighting westwards until the Afrika Korps had finally surrendered. They had suggested he could go back to the UK – a cushy billet at the moment – until his regiment was rebuilt for the invasion – that was something, he knew, which might take years. He turned that down too and volunteered to return to Italy to wait for the new assigment. Like all old sweats, the front had become more of a home than the seductive fleshpots of the Home Front. After this first successful, if costly, landing on the

European mainland, he suspected that the powers-that-be were sounding him out for a new task and it could only be behind enemy lines.

Wintle's next action seemed to confirm the suspicions that he had harboured ever since he had reached this HQ from Sicily three days before. The former said, "Too noisy in here." He grinned, but his cold blue eyes didn't light up. "Smells too much of naked power as well, old man. Shall we step outside for a chat and a breath of fresh clean air?"

It wasn't an invitation, but an order. Pitman rose immediately. Outside, Colonel Wintle waited till the yard had cleared a little of the latest batch of seriously wounded waiting to be flown to the hospitals of Messina in Sicily for urgent treatment. "The price of victory," he murmured, as they watched the wounded on their stretchers, most of them gratefully unconscious, but with here and there some sitting bolt upright on the blood-soaked stretchers, eyes popping out of their heads, screaming orders at men who were dead already. "Yes, the price of victory," he repeated, his clever face a mixture of compassion and contempt.

He cleared his throat and his voice rose. "All right, Pitman, you've volunteered for an assigment back of the lines. Well, here it is. We're going to drop you behind the lines in the Milan area. Your cover to the reception committee will be that you are working with them to expedite the escape of POWs formerly in Eyetie hands. But you'll let it be known to the commanders of the *Brigata Rossa*, the communist partisans, that you are really a Russian officer, working in deep cover."

"Wheels within wheels, sir?"

"Something like that," Wintle said easily. His face hardened. "But don't underestimate the danger. It will be every

man's hand against you. The Italian Reds, Musso's new
fascists and naturally the Huns and their bloody Gestapo."

"I understand that, sir," Pitman answered equally gravely.
"But what is the real purpose of my mission? Half a dozen
other chaps who speak fluent Italian could do the job you
propose."

"Cunning bugger, aren't you, Pitman," his superior said
without rancour. "All right, here it is." Quickly he looked
from left to right to ensure that they weren't being overheard
before he continued with, "Well, as you realise, old Winnie
Churchill has compromised himself somehow or other.
Musso has the papers that can prove that. Naturally if it
comes down to cases, the wop won't hesitate to use those
papers to save his precious skin. We want to be ready to
strike when that time comes – and you'll be the one to make
the decision. After all, you'll have a whole brigade of Eyetie
spies to give you the wire in advance – the *Brigata Rosso*."

Pitman nodded his understanding and said quietly, "And
what is to be the nature of this – er – *strike*, as you call
it, sir?"

The big Colonel with the dark Jewish features took
his eyes off the medical orderly sweating and cursing
profusely, as he tried to slit the windpipe of a writhing,
frantic soldier, his face purple as he choked to death. Next to
him, another stretcher-bearer was quietly vomiting into his
pudding-shaped helmet. It was a little pastiche of the horror
of war. "*Strike?*" he said finally, in a voice that seemed a
long way off.

"Yessir."

"I see. By strike I mean, Pitman . . ." He hesitated
momentarily as the wounded soldier fought to sit up for
one last time, his hands clawing the air, fighting off Death
itself ". . . kill him."

"*Kill him?*" Pitman gasped with awe.

"Yes, without Musso the papers would be valueless. They might have come from anywhere – be forgeries, for that matter. No, Musso and those Churchill Papers go together. See, if the crunch comes, that they don't."

For a moment there was silence, then Colonel Wintle said, "Come on, Pitman, let's see if we can cadge a stiff drink from the Yanks. Wash this mess away, what?"

Pitman didn't respond. He took one final look at the tableau of death over the other side of the bloody, muddy courtyard, and told himself it should be of some significance. But even as he did so, he knew it was of no significance at all, absolutely none.

Mr Yates And Colonel Pitman

Outside it was snowing hard, a relentless solid white sheet that flowed by the chateau's great window as if it would never cease. The morning had that muted, heavy feeling about it that always followed snow. Even the crunch of the odd car on the hard-packed village street seemed distant, as if taking place in some other village. In their stalls the frozen animals called miserably, great clouds of steam from their breath emitted periodically from the open door, as the farmer rattled his buckets and churns prior to milking the animals huddled together for warmth.

On the big bed, Colonel Pitman closed his eyes fiercely and concentrated on the task on hand. These days it had become hard work, but the maid, Paola was very kind and patient with him, muttering encouragement and supposed cries of delight every few minutes at the progress she told him he was making. She ran her little hand gently over the great scars that disfigured his body. "Poor Colonel," she said in Italian, the language they always used together privately. "How you have suffered. And for what?" She pulled a face in that unique Italian way which meant that life wasn't fair to good people.

He gave a little laugh and pulled her cunning little hand away. "Life isn't fair. Otherwise you wouldn't have to labour like this on me."

She returned his laugh and quoted the motto which appeared above every Italian church, "Labour and pray", adding, "but it is such sweet labour, Colonel, and I don't need to pray. It will work."

At that moment his heart went out to the beautiful girl and he would have given his right arm to be young, strong

192

and virile again so that he could return what she was giving him, a man three times as old as she.

Then he forgot the little Italian maid, the snow, his future after what he would have to do this day and the fate of the man two bedrooms away, still asleep presumably and possibly happy that he could go back to his editor with enough information to offer to gain himself a fat bonus cheque. For a few minutes he was concerned solely with his own pleasure, the exquisite pleasure she was giving him. Then it was over and she was stroking his damp brow soothingly, whispering sweet nothings, her dark oval face full of love. "I have given you pleasure, caro mio?" she said faintly.

He nodded his agrement, hardly able to get the words out, his pleasure was so great. "Yes . . . yes . . . much," he gasped. "You are very kind to such an old man. What have I done to deserve you? I—"

But she smothered the rest of his words with a wet gushing kiss before rising hurriedly and padding nakedly across the wooden floor to fetch his cheroots and 'medicine'. "Drink . . . smoke," she encouraged him. "You have done so much, suffered so much, been so patient. You deserve pleasure."

He accepted the drink tamely, although it was only eight in the morning. He couldn't disappoint her and spoil her obvious pleasure at his relaxed appearance. "We shall go back to Sicily – to my estate," he lied to her after a while.

She shivered melodramatically. "Away from this snow. Ugh." She shivered again. "We will be happy, caro mio."

"Of course we shall," he agreed, lying all the time. "I don't care what people will say. You will be my wife and in charge of my estate like one of those rich chickens from Rome, all furs and rings." He smiled and she smiled with him.

193

"*Such things don't matter, as long as I have you,*" *she said fervently and he knew the former little peasant girl, turned whore, was speaking the truth. He sighed inwardly. Of course that wouldn't be – he'd be dead before then. But he had made provision for that. She and Leon, the other servant, would be relatively rich people by Sicilian standards under the terms of his will and they would have the estate. They could turn that into money, too. No, they had served him loyally in life; he would do the same for them in death.*

Gradually she helped him to get into his clothes, the warm ones, for she knew something of his plans for this day, though not all or she would try to stop him. "*What do you intend with the Englishman?*" *she asked finally as she put his arms through the sleeves of the* Joppe, *the thick three-quarter length outer coat that the local farmers wore in winter.*

"*To get rid of him,*" *he replied hastily, not wanting her to ask any more about Yates's limited future.*

"*Will that be the last of him?*"

"*I hope so. Last night I told him enough to keep him satisfied. By the time he isn't, we shall be in Sicily and there we have – er – friends.*" *He laughed. She did, too. She knew his friends. No one in his right mind would want to rub* them *up the wrong way.*

"*What did you tell him?*" *she asked, beginning to dress herself, taking her time, although she was very cold.*

As he watched her draw on the sheer black silk nylons, pulling them up her shapely legs very slowly and tauntingly he answered, not taking his gaze off her for a moment, "*I told him what I knew of the origin of the Churchill Papers, what happened to them during the last month of the War and—*" *he hesitated; he didn't want her to know anything*

*which might cause her trouble in the years to come "—of
the events nearly ten years later in Venice."*

*"But that was so long ago," she said, lowering her upper
body so that her breasts fell exactly into the cups of her
black bra.*

*He waited, gaze fixed on her hypnotically while she a
patted and fiddled until she had got them right before
saying, "Yes, but what you do not know is what happened
thereafter."*

"What—"

*He held up his hand to stop her; she needed to know
only just enough. "Just let me tell you what happened to
the papers in April 1945. The rest you must imagine for
yourself."*

*She pouted a little, stopped dressing obediently enough
and, settling down on the edge of the big rumpled bed,
pulling part of the thick feather duvet over her legs, she
listened.*

"The commanders of the Brigata Rosso *decided to shoot
Mussolini in the third week of April. The Western Allies, you
see, Paola, had crossed into the Po valley, the Germans were
about to surrender and so the Reds of the Brigade wanted to
take a decisive step which would show the populace that the
communists were in charge in the north. They felt they could
swing a Red republic in that area now that everything was
in a state of confusion and no one seemed to be in charge
save themselves. Besides," Pitman added staring out of the
window at the falling snow, but not seeing it. Instead his
mind's eye was on the dramatic events of that parched
sunny spring when he had been young, "they were being
encouraged from other sources to dispatch the ex-Duce as
a traitor before the Allied military authorities arrived and
took charge in Milan."*

195

She noted the point, wondered who these mysterious
'other sources' could be – though she could guess who –
but said nothing. For her the old Colonel, who had once been
her grandmother's lover, too, in the War and afterwards,
could do no wrong. For him she had done everything, even
gone to bed with that swine of a newspaperman.

The old man's voice grew in excitement as he recalled
that last month, when he had been at the centre of the events
which would change the history of southern Europe. He
remembered the tension as the various factions raced to take
over the vital area, with the Red Army and their puppets of
Tito's partisans waiting in the wings in Yugoslavia to carry
out Moscow's commands for them. There had never been
another time like that; and there never would be again.

The Fiat manned by the partisan killers had swung round
the hairpin bend into the cobbled main square of the village
where the Duce was hiding with his mistress. Hurriedly the
SS under Schwarz scattered and went into hiding. Three
old women with their sackcloth skirts tucked into their long
knickers at the communal washing trough ceased slapping
the wet clothes against the stones and waited open-mouthed
for what was to come. Up above in the scrub and stunted
olives, he watched them all, fingering his pistol, like an
excited spectator in an antique amphitheatre. The sun beat
down relentlessly.

In his hiding place Schwarz hissed something to his bunch
of SS men, who had guarded Mussolini so long, but at
this stage of the War were no longer prepared to die for
him – or any one else for that matter. Schwarz looked
worried. Every now and again he touched the leather
bag – and it could only be the celebrated one belong-
ing to Mussolini – as if to reassure himself that it was
still there.

The Fiat skidded to a halt. Two men, obviously leaders, got out. Both were dressed flamboyantly with the red kerchieves of the communist partisans around their necks and both were heavily armed. Without hesitation they headed for the humble house to which Mussolini and his mistress had fled once their German SS escort had abandoned them to the partisans. Even as they marched, as if on parade across the bakingly hot piazza, Pitman knew they were going to kill the Duce.

Mussolini knew it, too, as he watched them come towards the house, and accepted his fate fatalistically. Clara had eaten off the packing case which served as their makeshift table and had crawled back into the rumpled bed, naked save her French lace petticoat. He wondered what was going through her mind. Didn't she realise she had to abandon him now *before she suffered the same fate as he would?*

He pecked at his maize porridge and the slab of maize bread and mortadalla without interest, listening to the harsh stamp of his killers getting ever closer. His 'New Romans' were coming to kill him and there wasn't one damned thing he could do about it.

The taller of the two, clad in a leather jacket, flung the door open, Biretta pistol clasped to his side, ready for use. His hard gaze swept the room, taking in the numb Duce *eating his* polenta, *the frightened mistress tugging up the bedding to hide her breasts, the abandoned gear kicked in a corner.*

He relaxed when he saw there was no danger here. He bowed slightly and said as a kind of introduction, "Brigata Rossa. *Please come with me,* Duce. *Your life is in danger."* *He looked at the terrified girl.* "You, too, Miss."

"I have no knickers on," Clara Petacci said somewhat stupidly.

Mussolini groaned. This was not the way a Roman should go to his or her death. 'I have no knickers on.' There was no style in the words. But he said nothing.

"Put them on," *the man in the leather jacket commanded.*

She did as he commanded, wriggling into the silken undergarments. The partisan did not even attempt to look away. It was then that Mussolini really knew they were going to kill them.

Five minutes later Mussolini, for some reason carrying a case (though he knew he would not need its contents ever again), appeared at the door of the house, his dark eyes squinting against the slanting rays. Behind him Clara Petacci followed, trying to comb her hair with her fingers. To Pitman, watching, she seemed flustered but not worried. Why? he asked himself. Had they been told nothing would happen to them if they behaved themselves?

Suddenly he was anxious. He had suggested to the partisan leaders last night in Milan, when the overwhelming decision had been made, that nothing should be said or done that should make the captives uneasy until they were in that safe place where it would happen. Then they had all been full of confidence. But he knew his Italians. Some of them were very brave individualists, but the mass performed best in a mob, where they could be egged on by the others and would be afraid to lose their macho image by backing off. Now these two would-be killers might be having second thoughts. What was he to do? Ensure that the assassinations were carried out or concentrate on Schwarz and the all-important case containing the Churchill Papers?

Pitman frowned hard. It was a damnable decision to be made at a moment's notice, but it had to be done: Mussolini or the papers. Down below, the driver started the Fiat and gunned the engine impatiently. The other two pushed in the ex-Duce and his mistress, with Clara crying now in a sad, silent, heartbroken way. He made his decision. Without Musso, the papers, wherever they landed, would not be of such great importance. He'd follow and ensure that Mussolini really was assassinated. It was vital for the Western Allies that he should not be brought to trial where he might well reveal his secrets in open court. At this moment, with Stalin and the communists breathing down their necks all over Europe, it wouldn't be politically opportune to have such secrets about dealings between the Western democracies and the central European fascist powers disclosed to the world.

As the Fiat began to move away, he swung himself hastily over the pillion of his battered motorbike and kick-started it into life. In their hiding place, the SS were alerted at once. They turned, startled, and seeing him depart, knowing instinctively that he had been watching them too, they fired a few wild shots after him. But he dodged them easily, zig-zagging wildly down the dusty tracks, bouncing over rocks at high speed so that within seconds he had turned the bend in the goat path and was gone.

Five minutes later he caught up with the killers. As he had suspected they hadn't gone far. Just far enough to carry out the murder out of earshot of the village and curious eyes.

He turned the engine off, the noise of his approach drowned by an Allied dive-bomber plastering the next village up the road, still held this hot April day by the retreating Germans, confused to a man, abandoned by their officers, uncertain of what to do, where to go and whether to fight. He left the bike and crept cautiously down the steep track between the tightly packed vines almost to where the little

199

group stood in front of a shuttered summer villa, its high white walls topped by a tall privet hedge.

The man in the leather jacket went a few yards up the road, sticking closely to the wall, while the other covered the two prisoners with his little pistol. They remained silent. Clara had ceased crying and was looking around her almost curiously, while Mussolini stared ahead stonily, as if he were already reconciled to what had to come.

The man in the leather jacket came back and nodded to the other one. He got down to the dreadful business of the execution straightaway. "By order of the High Command of the Volunteer Freedom Corps," he galloped away with the words, without feeling or pace, like a schoolboy who had learned something he didn't quite understand by rote, "I have been charged to render justice to the Italian people—"

Clara's shrill scream stabbed into the gabble of words, as she realised what they meant. "You can't kill us," *she cried out.* "You can't do that!"

"Move aside," the man threatened, jerking the muzzle of his pistol in her direction, "or we'll kill you first."

Next to him the one in the leather jacket, the sweat streaming down his contorted face, raised his machine-pistol. Watching them, Pitman dug his nails into the palm of the other hand painfully. This was the moment of truth. The man squeezed the trigger of the little machine-gun. Nothing happened! *He tried again. Still nothing. The gun had jammed.*

Cursing angrily, the would-be assassin tore his pistol from its leather holster and fired. A dry click. Again the weapon had jammed. Pitman told himself Mussolini's proverbial luck was holding out, even now at the eleventh hour. "Give me your damned gun!" the partisan yelled at his companion.

As the latter fumbled with his pistol, Mussolini started to undo his grey-green German Army tunic slowly. "Shoot me in the chest," he commanded slowly and the watching Pitman thought for the first time that behind Mussolini's bombast there was indeed something of the old Roman stoicism that he had always admired. But even as he said the words, a frantic, hysterical Clara grabbed for the pistol's muzzle.

Almost instinctively the crazed partisan fired. At that range he couldn't miss. She fell soundlessly, shot through the heart, still clutching a sprig of the flowering creeper she had picked up nervously when they had first stopped here. She lay there, her blood staining the dust at their feet. The killer didn't hesitate. Face contorted with rage and frustration, he fired two bursts at the one-time dictator. Mussolini yelled with pain as the bullets ripped open his body. He pitched forward, dead before he hit the dirt.

For one long moment, a great echoing silence reigned. In the hall of the villa the three hidden women who had witnessed the bloody slaughter huddled together, shaking and speechless. Faintly, very faintly, the thunder started to rumble over the mountains . . .

It seemed a long time before Paola said anything, as she sat there at the edge of the bed in that big cold, soulless room. In the end it was the old man who broke the brooding silence with, "Well, Paola, you know something of what happened to the Mussolinis in the last week of April '45."

She nodded. "I suppose everybody, young and old, does in Italy." She frowned. "How they strung them up – the mob in Milan – and all the rest of it . . ." her young voice trailed away to nothing and he told himself she didn't know the half of it. The mob taunting the dead, poking sharpened sticks at the two corpses, hanging upside down by their ankles from the girder outside the Milan garage, as they might wild animals, checking if they were really dead; old crones squatting with their knickers around their skinny ankles, urinating into Mussolini's gaping mouth; the grinning men ripping aside Clara's baby-blue silken knickers and running their hands between her legs so that they could boast later that they'd 'touched up' his 'woman'; the savage beatings of the former leader until his face was a bloody unrecognisable mess . . ." He cut the scene out of his mind. It was unworthy of the human race, even when it involved a man like Mussolini who had had plenty of innocent blood on his hands.

"And now?" she asked, changing the subject a little desperately, as if she knew what was going through her lover's mind at that moment. "What are you going to do with him?"

But before Colonel Pitman could reply, Leon appeared at the door, as noiselessly as ever. He gave a polite little cough, hand cupped in front of his mouth, as if he were hiding a set of bad teeth and said, "Sir, he asked me to inform you that he'll be ready for the trip to Liège in thirty minutes or so." He looked hard at his master, as if he wondered if the master would make some comment on what had to come. But Colonel Pitman didn't respond save to say, "Thank you, Leon. I think that – er – everything that can be done, has been done. The matter is almost closed . . ." Outside it started to snow once more.

Part Five

END RUN

"In August 1951 Mr Churchill travelled from London to Venice," Pitman said carefully, not looking at his companion, who was hanging on his every word; for he had not expected disclosures at this stage of the game.

"It was a journey which I need not tell you surprised a great number of people—"

"The British elections?"

"Yes, he was in the middle of the election game and it looked, after Labour had been in power since 1945, as if he was really in a position to unseat Major" *– Pitman couldn't forego that 'Major' –* "Atlee's government. So why did he go to Italy just then?"*

There was no reply (for obvious reasons) and Pitman answered his own question. "Because Skorzeny had suddenly turned up again, apparently out of nowhere after his mysterious escape from the Americans back in '48, and was making threatening noises. Churchill knew there was going to be a major attempt at blackmail and in London the left-wing papers, the* News Chronicle, *the* Daily Herald, *all those left-wing rags now long defunct,"* he smiled, again unable to forego hurting his companion in the back seat of the poorly heated Rolls, *"were already baying for blood."*

"Do go on. After all, this is straight from the horse's mouth. You were present at the Albergo Sole, where they met?"

That startled Pitman. He knew the name of the hotel even, that discreet third-rate hotel, which catered for poorer tourists. The newspaperman had done his homework well; it was time he was dealt with before he became too much of a threat. "Yes," he replied. "I was there. I did the interpreter *bit. Skorzeny tried his pathetic English, but the PM to be wouldn't have it. Indeed he wanted to have as little as possible to do with the 'Austrian crook', as he called Skorzeny."*

The other man nodded impatiently. They were leaving the low ground near the border river, the Our, and were heading into the hills. The snow was becoming dangerous and Leon had to slow down. Fortunately he knew the area like the back of his hand. That helped. "So?"

"So," Pitman echoed. "Well, Churchill indicated that Skorzeny should get on with it – state his price for the papers. He didn't want to waste any time on a man he regarded as a war criminal. Remember what he thought of the Huns in those days – they're either at your feet crawling, or they're at your neck, trying to strangle you." He laughed tonelessly. The old car was grinding its way up the slope in second gear, sliding and skidding in the new snow all the time. There wasn't another car in sight. They might have been the last people alive in the world.

"That was it all along, eh, Pitman?"

"Yes."

"And what was Churchill supposed to be buying? How good was the blackmail after all those years – it was blackmail, wasn't it?"

The old man nodded gravely. If he objected to being addressed as 'Pitman', he didn't show it. He concentrated on the task at hand, as Leon fought to reach the head of the minor road before they got stuck in this godforsaken place. "Apparently – according to the papers in Skorzeny's possession – Churchill had continued to correspond with Mussolini through secret channels for three years after Italy and Britain had gone to war. Churchill had even offered Mussolini the French African colonies, parts of the Cote

*d'Azur if Italy would turn against Hitler and get out of
the war against the Allies. As you rightly said, he was
even writing to Mussolini about evacuating Africa while
we were losing 13,000 men at El Alamein . . ." His voice
trailed away to nothing, as if, for the first time, he realised
the enormity of Churchill's deeds in writing to the enemy.*

*"And what was Skorzeny going to do with that info,
Pitman, if Churchill refused to play ball with him?"*

*Pitman shrugged. "One didn't need to possess a crystal
ball. Remember this was the height of the Cold War. Such
revelations would completely discredit him and the rest of
the so-called democratic leaders. All those fellow travellers,
who still haven't stood up seven years after the Berlin Wall
fell and confessed they had backed the wrong horse – you
know, the parlour pinks, the university pundits—"*

*"No lectures, Pitman," the other man cut in crudely.
A sweating Leon had nearly reached the top of the little
road. Soon they'd be travelling over Mount Rigi, the highest
spot in Belgium, heading for Eupen and the* autoroute *to
Liège. Pitman started to relax and enjoy other's obvious
discomforture. "And Churchill would lose the election to
Labour, too," he turned the knife in the wound cruelly.
"It would take an age before his beloved Tory party would
be taken seriously again, wouldn't it?" he sneered.*

*Pitman said nothing and the younger man said, "You
might as well tell me all of it now, Pitman. I think it'll
mean my editor, tight wad that the sod is, will give you
another couple of grand. He might even ask you to give
a personal interview . . . put you on telly with a couple of
those snart-arse Oxbridge profs on the make."*

*Inwardly Pitman shuddered at the very thought, but still
he played along with him. He had nothing to lose. He had
his plan and whatever he said now would never go any*

further than the old Rolls. So what did it matter what he told him now? "What did Skorzeny want? As soon as Churchill was re-elected, he wanted Churchill to put pressure on the Americans to make them and the Huns release war criminals – his old pals of the the 'Adolf Hitler Bodyguard', von Dodenburg, even the lowly Captain Schwarz," Pitman grinned for some reason. "I've mentioned him. He was Skorzeny's spy and stooge in the Mussolini camp. In essence, Skorzeny wanted those Nazi killers and adventurers released who might well form the nucleus of a Fourth Reich in the newly founded and very vulnerable Bundesrepublik."

At his chair near the window, overlooking the canal, a hitherto silent Churchill took his unsmoked Double Coronna out of his mouth and cleared his throat significantly. The Austrian started slightly. He broke off in mid-sentence and stared at the ageing politician.

Churchill's features were stony and unwinking.

Pitman reacted at once. It was as they planned. "Herr Skorzeny," he said to the man, a moment or two ago fully in charge of the situation in the hot little hotel room, now puzzled and uneasy. "I wonder if you would come to the window for a moment."

Wordlessly Skorzeny did as commanded, as Churchill bent his head and concentrated on poking a hole in the end of his cigar. He looked out. The street in the afternoon heat seemed listless and deserted; presumably everyone was taking a siesta, even the tourists. Then Skorzeny caught sight of the old-fashioned French Peugeot driving at a snail's pace down the centre of the street parallel to the canal. He frowned. Was this what the Tommies wanted him to see? If so, what did it mean? He

looked out of the corner of his eye at the other two.
Nothing.

Pitman enlightened him a moment later. "A little patience,
Herr Skorzeny. An old friend of yours, brought from Werl
Prison in the *Bundesrepublik* especially to see you."

Skorzeny's frown deepened. "Friend? What has this got
to do with—" He broke off suddenly. The long car had
stopped. A big burly man got out, one hand buried deep
in his right pocket. Carefully he looked up and down the
street. Satisfied, he nodded and another big man got out.
He, too, had his hand in his pocket. Skorzeny didn't need a
crystal ball to know that they were both cops, but what were
they doing here now? Were they Churchill's bodyguard? He
didn't think so. Churchill had had one solitary bodyguard
for years now and Skorzeny had checked; he hadn't flown
with the drunken old sot from London to Venice.

"Now look closely," Pitman urged, a cold smile on his
lips. Behind him Churchill kept his head down, seemingly
totally engrossed with his cigar. "Your friend—"

"What friend?"

"Patience, Skorzeny, you'll see in half a moment," Pitman
soothed him. "As I was saying, your friend from the old
days has been a bit naughty in prison of late. To be
exact, he stabbed a fellow prisoner to death last month.
Homosexual jealously. They will engage in these silly
passionate affairs behind prison walls. I'm afraid that as
we still have jurisdiction over Werl, he'll have to hang for
it, especially as the young German he killed was one of our
stooges." He shrugged. "But perhaps it's all for the best."

Now Skorzeny looked totally confused. Yet he could not
find the words to express his confusion. Instead he watched
the activity around the car, as if mesmerised into silence.

The two cops took one last look up and down the bakingly

hot street, and then said something to a man in the back seat. He barked something and next moment a familiar figure stumbled out onto the pavement, his hands cuffed behind his back. For a moment or two he stood there, wavering in the blinding light of the sun. One of the guards dug him in the ribs – hard – and pointed to the window of the Albergo Sole. Reluctantly he looked up – and Skorzeny gasped. "Why," he stuttered, "it's . . . the interrogator—"

"Yes," Pitman said calmly, "your old employee, Schwarz, the man who dutifully handed the Churchill documents to you—"

The PM looked up at the mention of his name, but as he couldn't understand German and the drift of the conversation, he bent to his expensive Cuban cigar once more.

"I'm trying to save him now," Skorzeny said a little desperately.

"Too late," Pitman said harshly, iron in his voice. He looked down at Schwarz, who appeared totally bewildered, wondering why he was here in Venice. He remembered that keen-eyed young *Luftwaffe* interrogator who had frightened him so much back in the makeshift farmhouse prison below the Gran Sasso and wondered at the change. Now Schwarz was flabby and pale from years of prison and prison rations, the dark hair of that jet-black cowl already greying and thin. The years had taken their toll. If it came down to cases, the man below would say and testify anything they wanted. But it would be better, he told himself, if it never came to that.

"Herr Skorzeny," he said very formally, taking his eyes off the poor victim below, "I have a proposition to make to you."

"Yes, what?" the man answered hesitantly, as if he were no longer sure that he had held the advantage in his hands, as big and capable as they were.

"You are living on borrowed time, Skorzeny." It was a statement of fact, not an opinion.

Suddenly Skorzeny looked scared. The man who had rescued Mussolini, had been called 'the most wanted man in Europe' by General Eisenhower, the Allied Supreme Commander in Europe, actually trembled. "I don't understand," he quavered in a voice he hardly recognised.

"Then I shall tell you."

Below the two cops were guiding a shaky Schwarz to the side of the canal where he looked across the gold-tinted surface of the water in complete bewilderment.

"So far, Skorzeny, you have enjoyed the protection of the American CIA and the Egyptian Secret Service—" Pitman held up his hand to stop Skorzeny saying something. "Don't deny it. Your file is fully documented. Now, Skorzeny, what do you think would happen to you, if the protection of those two agecies was removed?"

Down below the two cops had backed Schwarz against the balustrade, his pale pudgy face full of fear.

"The Israeli Mossad would be on to you like a shot, Skorzeny. They have plenty of scores to pay off against you for all those Nazi scientists, spies and the like that you imported into Egypt to work against the Jews."

"But the *Amis* would never buy that," Skorzeny said urgently, dark eyes wild. "Egypt is the OIA's main bulwark against the spread of communism in the Middle East and Africa." His gaze flashed from Pitman to Churchill; it was almost a look of appeal. Neither of the two Englishmen responded.

At the balustrade, the two cops were holding Schwarz tightly, one of them with a great silenced pistol in his hand. In the car the driver was revving the engine urgently, as if he couldn't drive off quickly enough.

"But the Jews will kill me," Skorzeny almost screamed, his whole body trembling now. "You couldn't do that to me—" The words froze on his lips. Down below the cop had fired. Schwarz sagged at the knees like a newly born foal. Next moment the two of them heaved the dead body over the balustrade. Schwarz hit the water with a splash and even before the driver had thrust the car into first gear, the two cops were clambering inside and they were moving off. A second later they had hurtled around the corner, leaving the street bare and brooding in the heat behind them, no trace of what had happened there, as if it had never taken place . . .

"Christ Almighty," Yates breathed out incredulously. "You didn't, did you?" he asked in a tiny voice.

Pitman nodded slowly and stiffly. "The threat worked and that was the end of Herr Skorzeny. Soon after he went to South America to supervise the Nazi gold and keep a watchful eye on Eva Perón . . . but that's another story you might have taken up."

Yates, aghast at what he had just heard, missed that 'might'. But by then it didn't matter. It was too late for the self-styled 'veteran newshound' to alter events in any way.

Pitman leaned back with a little sigh as Leon negotiated the bend from the village of Sourbrodt onto the main mountain road from Malmédy to Eupen. He said, "The snow hasn't settled so much here, Yates. I think, with a bit of luck, we'll make Eupen and the autoroute all right. For the Ardennes this place is comparatively flat, but dangerous," he commented a little like a tourist guide, while Yates's head raced at what he had just learned. "The locals call it the 'High Fenn'. There's deep swamp to both sides of

211

this road. In December '44 when the Huns launched their last airborne attack in support of their surprise offensive up here, more than one German transport plane disappeared completely on landing. Went right under in the swamp without trace. Remarkable, what?"

Yates didn't seem to be listening. His bewilderment had changed to delight. Not only had he a tremendous wartime story, but he'd got a smashing case of the currently fashionable sleaze. The old bugger Churchill having some poor sod bumped off in order to win a general election. Nobody in Britain had gone that far yet. "But what happened to the papers – those letters between Musso and Churchill?" he asked.

Pitman didn't seem to hear. Instead he said, "Let's have a leak stop next to that boarded-up kiosk. It'll be the last place we can park before we get down to Eupen and, you know, Yates, old men need to go a lot." He chuckled as if at his own dilemma, though there was no warmth in the sound.

"Okay," Yates agreed. "I could do with it myself. Must be this cold weather."

Pitman leaned forward and gave his order to Leon. The latter nodded his understanding, but frowned. Perhaps he was afraid they wouldn't be able to negotiate the snow and get back to the main road once more if they stopped.

They paused, engine still running, at the edge of the snowbound layby. Traffic had ceased for a while. A white wind careened across the high plateau, coming straight from Siberia, hurling the snow it brought with it at the ancient Rolls. Pitman got out stiffly. "Leon," he commanded, "see we're on the straight line, so we can come out without turning our wheels. Could get stuck like that." Leon, looking worried, did as he was ordered, while Pitman creaked his way into the vacant seat. "All right, Yates, you go first. Make it snappy. I'll follow, keeping the engine running while you take your leak."

Yates didn't argue. It was too cold to do so. Besides his mind was elsewhere than this remote Belgian plateau with the snow coming down in a solid sheet. He crouched in the shelter of the back of the old car, its roof already turning white with the snow beginning to settle on it immediately. He unzipped his fly. It was hellishly cold and he couldn't urinate straightaway. It was always the same with him in cold weather.

"All right," Pitman called, the windscreen clear. Outside, Leon, who had backed him into the layby, nodded his head, his eyes suddenly full of tears, though they weren't from the cold. Pitman wasted no more time. "You've had your day, old friend," he yelled to himself, his face almost youthful for a moment with the sudden wild excitement that surged through his body. He let out the clutch. The Rolls jumped. It started to move backwards.

"What in holy Christ is—" Yates shrieked and jumped backwards. There was no space to move to left or right. Pitman jammed his foot down hard on the accelerator. The tyres whined, throwing up a wild white wake of snow, blinding a suddenly terrified Yates. He flung up his hands, as if to ward off what was to come. To no avail. He stumbled and screamed. Arms flailing wildly, he went backwards over the slight incline. A moment later the heavy old car followed. With a great splash it hit the swamp. A huge gurgle. For a fleeting second it seemed it might rest on the bubbling, spluttering, shifting surface, but with a spurt of evil-smelling marsh gas, it went under, taking Colonel Pitman with it. Quickly, it disappeared. A series of obscene belches followed, as the air from the Rolls escaped, getting weaker all the time, till they vanished altogether, leaving *behind only the mournful howl of the wind sweeping that desolate, remote plain. Leon waited. In vain. He had seen the last of the old Colonel. He wiped the tears from his red-rimmed eyes with his hoary hand, crossed himself, turned and then began to trudge down the road to Eupen. In a matter of moments he had vanished altogether, leaving that bleak spot to lonely death – and memories.*